BOUND IN DEATH

CYNTHIA EDEN

Cover art and design by: Pickyme/Patricia Schmitt

Proof-reading by: Brenda Errichiello of Brenda's Eclectic Editing

DEDICATION

A very big thank you to Eden's Agents—you are all so amazing!! Thank you for being a part of my team!

PROLOGUE

Ireland, 200 years ago...

"*Please!* Don't kill him!" Keira McDonough's scream, high and desperate, rang out across the crowded chamber.

Her cry cut through the noise as easily as the silver blade that had just sliced into his chest. The blade that had stopped right at Alerac O'Neill's heart.

The men around him hesitated. No, these were not men. They were monsters. Vampires, hiding behind the guise of mere mortals. They wanted his blood. Both to drink it and to see it staining the stone floor beneath his feet as he died.

Perhaps that dark wish was only fair, considering the fact that he wanted their blood, too. *And I'll have it.* Alerac wouldn't meet death without taking those bastards with him.

But then *she* was there. Keira's blond hair whirled around her pale face as she shoved her way through the throng of vampires. They growled and flashed their fangs at her, but Keira didn't stop. She didn't fear the vampires gathered there.

She should.

"Lorcan…" She stared—her eyes wide and so damn blue that it almost hurt to look into them—at the man who'd just thrust that silver knife into Alerac's chest. "Don't do this. Please, I'm begging you!"

Keira should never beg. Especially not for his life.

Among her kind, she was a princess. A treasure. One that he'd tried to take.

"Don't," Alerac gritted out the word even as smoke rose from his chest. "Don't you beg him for *anything.*" The silver blade burned, destroyed—that was its purpose. It was a weapon meant to be used against his kind.

Another monster, hiding under the guise of a man.

Only his beast was far more vicious than most could imagine.

Keira's lips trembled, and she shot a quick glance his way before focusing on Lorcan once more. "I'll take his punishment."

The great room became dead silent. Every eye turned to Keira. Every eye, every ear, every fang.

"No," Alerac shoved the word out. "You can't!"

And *he* was shoved down to his knees. The knife was jerked from his chest and instead put to his throat.

Lorcan turned his head and pinned Keira in his sights. "His punishment is death. He came here, he *used* you, in order to get into our midst. To attack us from within." Lorcan Teague's voice cracked with fury.

The other vamps backed up in the face of his rage because Lorcan was the ruler. The leader of the vamp clan. A clan that Alerac had sworn to destroy.

He wanted these vamps to be nothing more than ash in the wind.

Except for her. Keira isn't like the others.

He'd learned that lesson too late.

The silver blade burned and cut along Alerac's throat. He wanted to tell Keira that Lorcan's words were a lie, that he hadn't been using her.

Only Lorcan wasn't lying. Why bother with a lie when the truth was just as brutal?

Alerac's plan had been simple enough, back in the beginning. Keira McDonough was the weak link in the vampire clan. The human who hadn't turned, not completely. She'd been born to the blood, but her transformation to full vampire hadn't occurred yet. He'd watched her from afar, because that was the only way *to* watch her.

The vampire princess. Locked away in her tower. Precious to her clan, so very valuable because of *what* she represented.

Hope.

She'd been locked away, but he'd always been good at picking locks. Getting to her side had been easy enough.

So had seducing her.

Keira had been his instrument of revenge. He'd hoped to use her to get killing close to Lorcan.

Only now, Lorcan was the one with the knife.

"I-I've started turning." Her voice was hushed. The room was filled — easily — with at least twenty vampires. All men. Female blood born vampires were incredibly rare.

That was why they held such value.

"When," Lorcan demanded.

"Y-yesterday."

Lorcan yanked the knife away from Alerac's throat and grabbed Keira. The vampire pulled her close, caught her chin in his hand, and tilted her face back so that he could stare into her eyes.

Alerac knew why Lorcan gazed so deeply into Keira's eyes. If Keira were truly turning, then gold should be spreading in her gaze.

The gold will be there. Alerac had already seen it for himself. His hands clenched as he pulled at the silver manacles that bound him. He no longer felt the burn on his wrists or ankles. Right then, rage was all he could feel. He wanted Lorcan's hands off Keira. He knew the vamp lusted for her — *but you won't have her. Not now. Not ever.*

"You *are* turning," Lorcan said as he held Keira's chin. Then he cast a hard, suspicious stare at Alerac. "Have you fed for the first time?" His features — frozen forever in a mask of youth that made him look as if he'd barely passed his twenty-fifth year — were hard with tension.

"Y-yes." Her stark whisper. "I've fed." Her gaze darted to Alerac.

She took my blood. The blood of a werewolf.

First, she'd given him her body. Trusted him as she had no other. He'd seduced her slowly, day by day. Week by week.

He'd taken her body. Deepened the connection between them.

Then *she'd* bit him. His blood had been the first that she ever tasted.

In turn, Alerac had taken her blood and discovered a rush of power that he'd never anticipated.

Lorcan's jaw locked. He lunged toward Alerac once more.

Alerac smiled at the bastard.

Aye, my blood, in her.

"He used you, Keira!" Lorcan snarled. Alerac's blood dripped from the knife gripped in Lorcan's left hand. "And yet you would give your life for him? *Why?"* His thundering voice echoed through the chamber.

The other vampires shifted nervously. When Lorcan was this enraged, people died. It was an understood fact.

Everyone there knew the pattern. Lorcan's love of blood and death was too well documented.

"Why?" Another bellow from Lorcan when Keira didn't answer quickly enough.

Alerac saw the faint movement of her throat as she swallowed. "Because I love him," Keira said softly, but with certainty.

Alerac's smile faded. Keira wasn't supposed to love him. He wasn't worthy of her love.

Now it was Lorcan who smiled. He shook his dark head. "You can't die for him, Keira. You have too much value to us."

That was right. Alerac eased out the breath that had frozen in his lungs. Keira couldn't, *wouldn't* die. Lorcan could continue his torture tactics, but he wouldn't be able to hurt Alerac for much longer. Alerac's pack was coming. They'd be there before—

"But you can take his punishment," Lorcan continued, all of the anger suddenly gone from his voice. Flat and cold, he said, "After all, you were the one to bring him in to our clan. A dog, walking among gods."

"You're no god," Alerac shouted at him. Lorcan was nothing, a blood drinker who lived off the fear he stirred. The werewolves were the truly powerful beings—both man and beast. Power and savagery in one dangerous package. And they didn't have to *feed* off others in order to survive.

Lorcan's dark eyes narrowed. "One hundred years. That's the penalty for treason in our clan. Imprisonment. Starvation. For one hundred years."

No, no, that wouldn't happen to Keira. His men were planning to attack the compound. They'd save Keira long before she suffered even a single night's pain.

Keira eased closer to Alerac. Her skin seemed to become even paler as she gazed at him. They'd sliced him, cutting into his body with that silver knife for hours, and they'd kept him manacled with silver so that he wouldn't be able to transform into the body of his wolf.

No transformation meant no healing.

They thought they were making him weak.

They were wrong. He was the alpha of his pack. There was no weakness.

Except her.

Keira's hand lifted. Her palm brushed against his cheek.

He'd had her under him, in bed, that very
night. He'd given in to his need one more time.
Made a desperate mistake.

Lorcan had found them.

Now Lorcan thought to make Keira pay?

"Don't," Alerac ordered her. The word was a
growl from his beast.

Her hand dropped.

Her smile broke the heart that he shouldn't
have. "I won't let you die." Her chin lifted. Her
bright stare cut toward Lorcan. "I will take the
punishment, but you have to promise me that
Alerac lives." Her voice grew louder. All watched
her with wide eyes. "No matter what else
happens, he *lives."*

"Why?" Lorcan's lips were still twisted into a
sly smile. "By the time you are free, he will be
long dead."

Because werewolves weren't immortal, not
like vampires. Not like their sworn enemies.

A battle that had raged for so long.

Blood. Death.

"Swear it, Lorcan," Keira pushed, her voice
even stronger now. "Vow it to me on the blood."

Lorcan's gaze returned to Alerac. Smug
vampire. "I vow it," he agreed easily enough.

Keira's shoulders slumped. She glanced back
at Alerac once more. Then she bent before him,
wrapping her arms around his shoulders and
bringing her lips close to his ear. "I know you did

not love me," she whispered, her mouth brushing against him. "But I loved you." Then she pulled back. Looked deep into his eyes.

The first time he'd seen her, he'd thought she was a dream.

A beautiful, perfect dream—a temptation.

A destruction.

Her lips pressed lightly against his.

"Take her," Lorcan ordered, voice booming.

Other vampires rushed to obey.

Keira was hauled back.

He stared up at her, desperate. Alerac wanted to tell her that help was coming, it was just hours away. *Hours? Or minutes?* During the torture, he'd lost track of time, and Alerac wasn't sure how long it would be before dawn arrived.

But if he told her about the others, then all of the vampires would be alerted to his plan. His men wouldn't have the element of surprise on their side. He had to protect his pack.

An alpha's job was always to protect the pack.

Shackles were put around Keira's wrists.

No.

He leapt to his feet with a roar, ignoring the silver and the vampires who tried to subdue him. The power of his beast beat within him. The sight of Keira, bound, enraged him. Not her. No one could hurt her. No one *would* hurt her.

The manacles broke from the walls. He lunged toward Lorcan.

But vampires could move fast, so very fast. Before Alerac could reach him, Lorcan's bloody knife was at Keira's delicate throat.

"If she loses her head, she will die easily enough." Lorcan's Irish brogue whispered through the words. A brogue that he picked up, and dropped, seemingly at will. Lorcan was centuries old. Some tales said that he'd been born a Viking and had journeyed to Ireland long ago, bringing hell with him. "Do you want her death on you?" Lorcan asked as he studied Alerac. "Seems so pointless, especially when we worked out a deal."

There was no fear in Keira's eyes. "Imprisonment won't kill me. It will hurt. I will suffer." She swallowed and pulled in a deep breath. "But I won't die."

And you won't be imprisoned. My men will have you free by dawn.

"All of this…because I killed a few of your dogs?" Lorcan's knife nicked Keira's throat. Her blood trickled down in a dark red line. "They should have known better than to tangle with me."

Vampires reached for Alerac. He threw out his chains, catching them across their faces. Snapping bones. Fighting. He couldn't attack Lorcan, not while he held that knife at Keira's throat, but he could go after the others. "They were my family!" The rage came then, building, swelling within him. The vampires had taken away what he valued, now it was his turn to destroy them. To wipe out their stronghold. To end their blood reign.

Because of Keira, his men now knew how to get inside the vampire's keep. With the light of dawn, they'd attack. The timing had been deliberate. Vampires were weakest during the day. The vampires would be weak, but the wolves would be at full strength. *How long is it until dawn?*

"They were family," Lorcan dismissed, a sneer twisting his face, "and now they're rotting in the ground."

Keira tensed. Then she spun around, moving fast—far faster than Lorcan had obviously anticipated. *Vampire speed.* Now that Keira was turning, she was coming into her vampire powers.

In a flash, she grabbed the knife from Lorcan, and she shoved it into *his* chest.

But silver wouldn't kill a vampire.

It would just make him *hurt*.

The other vampires swarmed around Alerac.

"Two hundred years!" Lorcan cried out. "You just attacked...your leader..."

"If I had my way," Keira said, as she stood before Lorcan, not backing down a bit, "you'd be dead."

Lorcan yanked out the knife. Tossed it to the floor.

Eight vampires held down Alerac.

"Keira?" The voice, stunned, male, came from the open doorway.

Keira's head turned at the call.

No, not now!

But, with his incredibly poor timing, Keira's twin brother had just appeared. Ryan stood in the doorway, his hands fisted at his sides. His hair was as golden as his sister's. His eyes as blue.

"Keira, what have you done?" Betrayal was on Ryan's face. Rage.

The vampires had all turned on Keira. While she—

She chose me.

His nails lengthened into claws as the beast pushed for freedom. The wolf within him was desperate to protect his mate.

My mate?

No, no, that couldn't be right. A werewolf would never mate with a vampire.

Fuck her, yes.

Use her, yes.

Mate?

Keira turned back toward Alerac. "I hope you…live a good life."

She'd traded two hundred years for his survival.

The beast howled inside of him.

"Ryan…" Lorcan ignored the blood that poured from his chest. "Your sister confessed to conspiring with the wolves. She has even agreed to be punished in the wolf leader's place."

Ryan rushed toward her. "Keira, you can't—"

"Imprisonment. Starvation." Lorcan licked his lips. "Two hundred years."

Ryan blanched. "Sh-she won't survive! You know she won't!"

"Then maybe she shouldn't have spread her legs for the wolf, and *then shoved a fuckin' knife in my heart!*" Jealousy and fury tore through Lorcan's words.

Alerac knew Lorcan had planned to wed Keira. He'd locked her away because he'd wanted her. Wanted the power that she represented.

Ryan grabbed for Keira. Pulled her against him. "Kill the werewolf!" Ryan ordered, voice thundering. "Just do it—*now!*"

But Lorcan shook his head. "I gave a blood vow. It's done. He lives, and so does she."

Ryan twisted Keira around in his arms.

Alerac's blood dropped onto the floor. The vamps would feed on him. He knew they wouldn't be able to resist the scent of all that blood much longer.

He wanted them to feed on him. His blood was laced with a special tonic — a poison just for them. He'd known that he would be captured that night. He just hadn't counted on Lorcan finding him just as Alerac drove into Keira's delectable body.

That whole capture bit should have come *after* Keira had been told to flee from that place. But Alerac's lust for her had been his downfall. He'd given in to his need once more.

And his perfect plan had gone to hell.

If Alerac had kept his hands off Keira hours before, then she would have escaped to safety.

Instead, she had just sacrificed herself for him.

Alerac's breath came out in low, hard pants. Keira would be fine. The punishment would never be carried out. He'd given orders to his men already — Keira wasn't to be hurt. Just in case he hadn't been able to convince her to flee, he'd made sure that his men knew their attack couldn't hurt her.

"Keira, you can't do this! You *can't!*" Ryan shook her. Her head snapped back.

Then she jerked away from him. "They aren't monsters." Her voice was low. Sad. "We are."

Ryan's eyes widened as he shook his head. "No." He rushed toward the vampire clan's leader. "Lorcan, please, don't do this! I'll do—"

"*Anything?*" Lorcan murmured.

Ryan nodded quickly.

Lorcan laughed. "There's nothing I want from you. Nothing I can't *take.*"

Another woman pushed through the crowd then. A pale woman with long, red hair and a twisting scar that wrapped around her neck. Jewels glittered on her fingers and power seemed to swirl in the air around her.

A witch.

Lorcan's witch.

The same witch who'd been at his side when Lorcan slaughtered nine members of Alerac's pack.

"But I can be merciful," Lorcan continued as the witch approached him. He reached for his witch's hand. "Shonna, my dear…"

She only flinched a little bit when he touched her.

According to the whispers, she'd tried to flee from Lorcan once. He'd retaliated by nearly taking her head.

She hadn't attempted to leave him again.

"Work up a spell," he ordered her softly as his gaze stayed on Keira. "Freeze her body so that she does not need air to breathe. Keep her aware, of every single moment. Let her know that time is passing, let the hunger for blood consume her as she remains motionless in her prison."

Shonna nodded. "It will be done."

No, it fuckin' wouldn't be.

Lorcan tapped his chin. "As I said, I am not without mercy."

Lying bastard.

"My vampiress must suffer during her imprisonment," Lorcan said. "For what is punishment without pain? But the instant she is free, then I want her to forget."

Lorcan's gaze slid to Alerac. To the vampires who were fighting so desperately to hold him down.

Keira.

"I want her to forget everything," Lorcan said as his shoulders squared. "*Everything*." Then he glanced at Ryan once more. "You see, she'll be able to recover. She'll be able to come back to us."

Hope flashed across Ryan's face.

"I won't come back," Keira vowed. "I won't be like you."

Lorcan laughed. "You already are."

A tremble shook the witch's body. Shonna's lashes swept down, concealing her gaze.

Lorcan stalked back toward Alerac. He knelt down, getting too close.

Your mistake.

"Keira *will* come back to us, and, by then, you'll be long dead."

But I am not dead yet.

Alerac's claws flew up. He scraped across Lorcan's cheek, digging deep into the vamp's flesh.

Lorcan screamed and jerked away. He glared down at Alerac, chest heaving.

"*You'll* be the one who is dead," Alerac promised him.

"No, I'll be the one mated to Keira while you are no more than a pile of bones." Lorcan swiped away blood. "Take her."

"No!" Ryan shouted.

The shout did no good. All of the vampires in that hall were loyal to Lorcan. Their allegiance did not belong to Ryan, to a man who'd been blood born, but was only now beginning his transformation into a full vampire.

Keira didn't fight the hands that grabbed her. Her eyes — still unafraid, still too trusting — met Alerac's, and that trusting gaze broke something in him.

Ryan rushed after her. After her…and the witch. Because Shonna had followed the group that took Keira away from Alerac.

The heavy, wooden doors closed behind them.

Alerac was left with about ten vamps who were all salivating for his blood.

Drink up. Fuckin' drink up. The faster they drank, the faster they'd die. He'd been sure not to let Keira sample his blood that night. But as for the others…

Drink your fill.

"I said you would get to live." Lorcan picked up the silver knife. Flashed his fangs. "But I never vowed that you would not suffer."

A vampire yanked back Alerac's head, forcing him to stare up at Lorcan's face.

The leader smiled. "I think I'll start with your eyes. After all, what good is a wolf that cannot see?"

Dawn would come soon. *Hours? Minutes?*

He could survive anything until dawn. He knew Lorcan would not kill him right away. All in the realm knew of Lorcan's love for torture. He never let any of his enemies die easily.

He made my family suffer for hours. Days.

Alerac had been gone, taken away by another battle. When he'd returned, there had been only decaying bodies waiting for him.

"I'm going to carve out your eyes, wolf. Then I'm going to carve *you* up. Slice by slice. When you're bleeding from a hundred wounds, we'll feast on you." The blade came toward him, but in Alerac's mind, he didn't see it. He only saw Keira.

Then he saw nothing.

But he felt plenty, especially when the vampires began to feed on him.

***

"What did they do to him?" The voice—low, rumbling, angry—came to him in the darkness.

Why was it still dark? Dawn should have come by now.

"Alerac? Blast Lorcan to hell. *Look at his eyes.*"

Then, rough hands yanked him to his feet.

"Alerac, Alerac, it's Liam. We got in, just like you said. We found the vampires. Half of 'em were passed out."

Because they'd feasted on his blood—just as Lorcan had promised. Drained him nearly dry.

They'd taken the poison right from his veins.

"A few got away, but we'll catch their scents. We'll hunt them," Liam swore.

Liam…the werewolf who was like a brother to him. The one who always had his back.

Alerac tried to force himself to speak. "K-Keira…"

"You need to shift. Do you hear me? *Shift now.*" The snap of command was in Liam's voice. So was the whisper of fear.

Only a shift would heal Alerac's injuries. Not just one shift, not after all they'd done to him.

A few hours…

There was much, much that could be done in that time.

Alerac shook his head and nearly fell back down to the stone floor.

"Get the silver *off* him!" Liam demanded.

He didn't feel that silver anymore.

But something hit the stone floor with a clunk. *The chains?*

"The silver's gone," Liam said as he pulled Alerac forward, forcing him to walk. "Shift."

He couldn't. He could barely sense the beast inside of him. There was something else that was more important. Something he needed.

The only person he could see in the darkness that surrounded him.

"K-Keira…" Her name was a broken rasp. They'd cut his throat, torn it with their fangs, and that weak rasp was all he could manage then.

Liam swore. "The vampire bitch? Look, we didn't hurt her. We didn't even *see* her."

She was all that Alerac could see. Her eyes had been so blue. So trusting.

There had been love in her eyes.

Love for a beast who'd betrayed her.

"Keira…" Saying her name made him feel stronger. Made the beast inside stronger.

"The lass is not here! She wasn't here when we arrived. Look, forget her — *shift!* Your eyes — they — they — "

He knew what they'd done to his eyes.

Just as he knew about all of the flesh they'd cut from him. Inch by inch. Slice by slice.

A growl built in his throat. They'd taken Keira. Sent her to be imprisoned? He had to find her. Had to find —

His bones began to snap. The wolf shoved and clawed his way to freedom as he pushed to get to the one thing he needed so desperately.

His knees gave way. He broke from Liam's grip and hit the floor. His claws scraped over the stones. He opened his mouth. Tried to call Keira's name once more.

But it was the wolf's cry that escaped from him. A long, mournful cry for a mate who wasn't there. A mate he hadn't recognized.

Not until it was too late.

Two hundred years...

CHAPTER ONE

Present Day

Someone was watching her.

It wasn't the casual, even flirtatious, stares that she sometimes attracted when she worked at Wylee's Bar. Sure, her skirt was short enough and her top tight enough to get plenty of second glances.

But this wasn't about her clothes. Or her figure. Or about some kind of fast hook-up between strangers.

I feel hunted.

Very carefully, Jane Smith put the empty beer pitcher on the bar. Then her gaze rose and locked on the long, stretching mirror that covered most of the wall behind that bar. In the mirror's gleaming surface, she could see the crowd that filled Wylee's.

And the man who watched her.

Goosebumps rose on her skin. The man was big, muscled, with huge shoulders that filled the doorway—and he was still standing just inside the doorway. He'd angled his body toward the shadows so that she couldn't clearly see his face, but she knew he was watching her. The realization was instinctive. Bone deep.

"Jane? Table four is waiting for you." More beer was pushed toward her.

She didn't move. She didn't want to head over and check on table four. She wanted to run, fast and far, from that little bar.

Because she was afraid.

In the last six months, she'd been afraid plenty. Countless times, she'd woken up at night, screaming, not even knowing why. She never dreamed when she slept. Just saw darkness. Total and complete.

But she feared.

The man in the doorway—*I'm afraid of him.*

"Jane?" The bartender and the owner of the place, Hannah Wylee, frowned at her. "Girl, you look like you're about to faint."

She felt that way, too.

But Jane forced herself to reach for the tray. To curl her hands around it and turn away from the bar and that broad mirror. She turned—

He was still in the doorway. So tall. The stranger had to be about six foot four. And those shoulders—they were truly brushing the sides of the old, wooden entrance to Wylee's Bar.

She wanted to see his eyes.

She was terrified to see them.

Jane lifted her chin, lifted that tray, and scurried through the crowd. It was a Friday night, and Friday nights were always busy. It was Miami—a city known for non-stop parties. Tourists, locals—everyone piled in on Friday nights.

It was only slightly past ten PM; the night was young. She wouldn't be escaping from this place until close to six that morning.

Bodies brushed against her. Hands that were a little too friendly tried to slow her down. Offers, invitations were thrown out to her. She ignored them, hurrying toward table four.

Only she didn't make it to the table.

She walked right into *him*.

He shouldn't have been able to get across the bar that fast. But he had.

Her tray bounced against him. Beer sloshed, and she had to do a frantic grab to make sure that the whole tray didn't go crashing to the floor.

Music beat around them. Voices rose and fell. Laughter filled the bar.

"I've been looking for you." His voice was deep. Rumbling. Tinged with the faintest of accents.

Her goosebumps got even bigger.

Look at him.

She made her gaze rise. Her eyes locked on his.

No, not *on* his. On the sunglasses he was wearing. Um, sunglasses, in a bar? *At night?* What was up with that?

Her attention shifted to his face. To the hard, square line of his jaw. A jaw that was clenched. His lips—sensual, a little cruel—were pressed into a thin line.

Her heart slammed into her chest. Breathing deeply got incredibly difficult. "Uh, if you'll just get a table…" Before they all filled up, "one of the other waitresses will be with you in a few moments." Because she was *not* taking his table. Mr. Sunglasses could just keep on walking right past her.

He took the tray from her. Dropped it onto a nearby table.

"What the hell—" One of the frat boys at that nearby table began.

But the man with the dark hair, midnight black and so very thick, wasn't paying the frat guy any attention. No, the stranger had stepped forward. He'd wrapped his hands around her arms and pulled her right against him.

"I've waited long enough." Growled. Those words seemed more animal than man.

Her heart wasn't racing right then—Jane could have sworn that it stopped completely.

Trouble.

Her gaze cast frantically around the bar. Hannah wasn't looking her way. And where were the bouncers? They should be there to help with situations like this one. No one was supposed to mess with the staff.

Breathe, breathe. She forced herself to take a few deep breaths. Her heart began its mad thumping once more. "I think…" His voice had been a growl. Hers was a squeak. "I think you've got me confused with someone else." And she pitied that poor woman.

His fingers tightened. Then he was moving — cutting his way right through the crowd and hauling her with him.

Finally, *finally,* Hannah glanced up and saw her being dragged across the bar. Hannah's mouth dropped open in surprise even as her green eyes widened in alarm.

Yeah, Jane was feeling pretty dang surprised and alarmed, too.

Help me. Jane mouthed. Then she screamed it. But the music was pumping, the crowd was already shouting, and her scream did *nothing.*

She tried to twist out of the guy's hold, but there was no give to him at all. He didn't even seem to notice her struggles.

"Curtis! Sean!" Hannah yelled, calling out for the bouncers.

But her stranger had Jane at the back door. He shoved that door open and dragged her outside. The night air was hot. Thick.

She tried to pull away from him once more. Not happening. The guy's grip was unbreakable. He was strongest thing that she'd ever seen.

He pushed her against the brick wall of the building. Caged her there. "You should have come to me. As soon as you were free."

He was insane. "I'm not—"

His lips crashed down on hers. His kiss was wild, rough. Almost desperate.

She shoved her hands against his chest.

He didn't step back.

Jane sank her nails into him.

He growled and just kissed her harder.

All she could hear was the frantic beating of her heart. Too fast. Shaking her body.

He wasn't letting her go. His kiss—she felt like he was consuming her.

Fear beat at Jane. So much fear.

Where was Curtis? Sean? She tried to scream again, but his mouth muffled the sound. Fine, maybe she'd just bite the jerk.

Only, before she could, his head lifted. Finally. Lifted and—

He licked her neck. "Missed you. So fuckin' much." His accent had deepened. What was that? Irish? It sounded like an accent she'd heard on TV once. "Never gonna let you go again."

"Yeah, buddy, you will." Sean's sharp voice. "You'll be letting her go right *now*."

She sagged against the wall.

"You'll let her go," another hard male voice. *Yes!* That was Curtis talking! She recognized his familiar Alabama twang. "Or, mister, that'll sure enough be the last mistake you ever make."

Jane sucked in a deep, desperate breath.

Her stranger — still with his sunglasses on — gave a rough sigh. "You don't want to get involved in this," he said to the men. He didn't even bother glancing over at them.

"Yeah, we do." Sean was adamant. "Jane there is our friend, and you need to get your damn hands off her."

The man, who held her in a grip of steel, tensed. His head cocked, and he seemed to study her behind his sunglasses. "Jane." He tasted the name, frowning. "*No.*"

She found her voice with a stutter. "Pl-please, let me go."

His body locked, the muscles tensing even more against her.

"Let her go." Curtis's voice was harder than Sean's, harder and even meaner. "Or I'll taze your ass."

The tazer was Curtis's weapon of choice. He'd told her once that he didn't like to get bloody unless he had to.

Blood made the ex-linebacker feel nauseous.

"*Last chance,*" Curtis snapped, his drawl thicker. People usually jumped when Curtis gave an order.

Very, very slowly, the stranger eased his grip on Jane.

She immediately ran from him and straight into Sean's outstretched arms.

A growl rumbled in the air.

"What the fuck?" Sean muttered. He shoved her behind his broad back. She was so glad that Sean was there. Tall, tattooed, with his gleaming bald head and the bulging muscles that normally made even drunk men give him a clear path — he was a truly beautiful sight to her scared eyes right then.

Only the more she studied him, Jane realized that Sean didn't look so intimidating right then, not when he was so near the mysterious male — the *crazy* male — in the sunglasses.

The man who'd held Jane, who'd kissed her so fiercely, turned to slowly face them. Curtis came to stand at Sean's side, a united front. Curtis was as tall as Sean, but leaner, and his hands were currently curled around a tazer.

The guy never made empty threats.

"You're not wanted at Wylee's any longer," Curtis told him bluntly. "So hit the road, and don't come back."

He wasn't moving.

And the knot in Jane's stomach was getting worse.

"Jane isn't your name." He spoke just to her. Seemed to focus only on her.

Her heart stopped then.

"Why do you lie to them?" He took a step toward her. "Why lie to me?"

Her fingers clutched at Sean's arm. He glanced back at her. "Do you know him?" Sean asked.

Her gaze swept over the stranger's face. The lamp posts behind the bar tossed light on him. "I've never seen him in my life."

He took another step toward her. *"Lie."*

Curtis lifted his tazer. "Man, I told you—"

The stranger lunged for him.

Curtis fired his tazer.

Only the tazer didn't actually *do* anything to the man in black. The shock should have hit him, immobilized him, but he didn't even slow down. He yanked the electrodes out of his chest, and in the next instant, he was in front of Curtis. One powerful fist drove into the bouncer's jaw.

Curtis flew back. Hit the ground.

"Get inside, Jane," Sean demanded. "Get back inside, *now.*"

Then Sean tried to attack.

He was on the ground less than a second later.

And Jane was running—too late—for that back door.

Hard hands caught her around the waist and spun her around. She was screaming, not even realizing the desperate sound came from her, until his hand flattened over her mouth, stilling her cries.

"Stop fighting me. I won't hurt you."

She was supposed to believe him? After he'd just downed those two bouncers with barely any effort?

And why hadn't the tazer worked on him?

Her breath was rushing out in desperate bursts from her nostrils.

He brought his head close to hers and he- Inhaled?

She held her body completely still, too terrified to even move.

She'd seen something just this on TV last week. One of those crime shows that she liked to watch. A guy had been obsessed with a stranger. He'd stalked her. Killed her.

Then the detectives had spent forty-five minutes tracking him down. Their tracking hadn't done the victim any good, though. She'd been dead before the first commercial break.

I don't want to be dead!

His head lowered over her throat, and, yes, the crazy guy was sniffing her. Sniffing her, then…licking her?

She shivered. A combination of fear and—no, no, it had to just be from fear.

"I would know you, anywhere."

Her lashes had closed. When had she squeezed her eyes shut? Jane forced them open now. He'd stepped back, but she could actually still feel him. Feel his lips—his tongue—on her throat.

His hands dropped from her. "What game are you playing?"

Sean groaned.

Jane shook her head. "N-no game. You've got me confused with someone else." Her words tumbled out too quickly. Desperation would do that to a girl. Make her talk fast. Make her shake and quake.

"No." He was adamant. And he didn't even look back at Sean and Curtis. Why would he? Not like they were a threat any longer. "I know my vampire when I see her."

For a minute, she actually thought she might pass out. Just fall right at his feet. Her arms wrapped around her stomach as she swayed. "V-vampire?" Then she shook her head. "You're crazy!"

Wait, that probably hadn't the smartest thing to say to the guy.

A muscle flexed in his jaw. "You think I don't know?"

"Vampires aren't real." She was edging cautiously toward the bar's back door. Just a few more steps, and she'd be able to rush inside.

This time, she'd try to not get her ass dragged back outside again.

Like that had worked so well the first time.

He laughed.

The sound stopped her.

His laughter was deep and rumbling and dark. And the man was scary—so terrifying to her. So why in the world did she find the sound of that rough laughter to be sexy?

Maybe I'm the crazy one.

"I know your secrets." His voice was low, almost taunting. "Every last one."

He can't.

"Stay away from me," she whispered.

His lips parted. Wait, were his teeth sharper? Those teeth, his canines, sure looked sharper to her. They appeared to be getting even more so by the minute.

"Am I having a nightmare?" The question slipped from her. It sounded as absolutely lost as she felt.

His fingers lifted. Smoothed lightly over her cheek. "I can take away all of your nightmares. I can make sure you never know another instant of pain or fear in your life again."

If only. "Look, mister, you're the thing scaring me the most right now."

His hand seemed so hot against her flesh.

"Please," she was begging, she knew it. "Just let me go."

The light from the lamp posts and from the back of the building bounced off his sunglasses.

She was glad she couldn't see his eyes. She didn't want to see them.

In the next instant, his hand had dropped from her cheek and he'd grabbed her right wrist. He lifted up her hand, staring down at her palm. "Your rose. It marks you." His hold tightened. "I *know.*"

Now he was obsessing over that weird red birthmark? Okay, sure, if you squinted, it did look like a rose, but so what? "Let me go," Jane said again. Her desperation was making her voice shake.

"For now." He released her and stepped back.

For now and *forever.*

She took a few frantic breaths. Hope stirred.

"I'm not what you think I am." She had to convince him. Had to get the guy to walk away. "I'm not a vampire. I'm not some kind of monster." *Though you sure may be.* "I'm just a normal human, okay? Your average woman. My name is Jane and—"

"It isn't." Snarled.

Okay. The guy obviously had quite a few issues.

"You think I don't know you? You think I don't know your scent? Your touch? Every fuckin' thing about you?"

She took another careful step toward the door.

Another groan sounded behind her stranger. Sean. A fast glance showed her that he was trying to rise. *Hurry, Sean. Hurry.*

"You can't know me," she whispered, hoping to keep the stranger's attention on her long enough for Sean to get more strength back. "We're strangers." Her frantic heartbeat seemed to be bruising her chest.

He smiled then. "Liar."

That smile—it flashed actual fangs.

"G-get away from her!" Sean's voice. The guy sounded winded, and when the stranger's face tensed, she knew he was about to attack again.

"Don't." She reached for him. Curled her hands around his arms. "Don't hurt them again." Because she knew that he could.

Would?

But he nodded.

Voices rose in the wind then. Others were heading that way—maybe to the parking lot that lay a few steps behind him. Hell, maybe they were just walking that way in order to get some action in the dark.

Either way, their audience was increasing.

And her stranger, after one long look down at the hands that held him, tilted his head back. He nodded, as if he'd made a decision. "I'll see you again."

Not if I see you first.

He backed away and actually seemed to just…vanish into the night.

That was good. The whole vanishing bit was really good. Because in the next instant, Jane's knees gave way and she hit the ground. Hard.

Vampire.

Oh, shit. Her secret was *out.*

***

He'd scared her.

Dammit, that hadn't been his plan. He was there to protect her, to make certain that her blue eyes — still the most beautiful eyes he'd ever seen — never showed a hint of fear again.

Only those eyes had been terrified.

Because of me.

She'd taken one look at him, and the woman calling herself Jane had paled. She'd trembled.

She'd tried to run.

The beast inside of Alerac had responded instinctively. After such a long hunt, there had been no other way for him to respond.

Chase. Claim. Trap.

Cage.

He'd wanted to grab onto her and hold her as tightly as he could.

But she'd stared up at him and acted as if he were a stranger.

Worse, a monster.

Well, what was fuckin' new there?

"Did you find her?"

He turned at the words, not surprised to discover Liam waiting for him in the darkness.

They were both well used to the dark. "Yes." The word snapped out from Alerac.

Liam waited on the edge of the small parking lot, his body reclining against the motorcycle behind him. "I don't see her."

Wasn't he the observant one?

"We come all this way," Liam murmured, "we look for so long, but we don't take her?" He shook his head. "That doesn't make sense to me."

"She was terrified."

Liam laughed at that. "When has fear ever stopped you?"

It hadn't. Only…*it's her.* This was different. This was the most important mission of his life.

The only thing that mattered to him.

Liam sighed and ran a hand through his dark hair. "We came here to see if she was the one."

The one who haunted him. Obsessed him.

"If she *was* the one, then we were supposed to take her. That was the plan, right?"

Like he needed to be reminded of this shit. It was *his* plan.

Alerac marched toward his own motorcycle. Climbed on the bike. "There were too many eyes here." He shouldn't have approached her in that bar. He'd planned…hell, he'd just planned to walk inside. To get a look at her. To catch her scent. To see if she was the nightmare who chased him every time he slept.

Am I having a nightmare? Her voice, so different from what he'd expected, whispered through his mind. No accent lightened her words. Fear had made them breathless and husky.

Yes, he'd intended just to watch her that night. But once he'd actually crossed the threshold of Wylee's Bar, when her head had snapped up and his eyes had locked on her...

Beautiful.

She was just as beautiful as he remembered.

Those high cheekbones. That heart-shaped face. The plump lips. The hair that was the color of the sun — a sun she'd once loved.

Barely five feet four, she'd always been small. Deceptively delicate, but curved in all of the right places. Places he'd touched and kissed.

One look and all he'd been able to think about was touching her again.

"But she fuckin' feared me," he muttered.

Liam whistled. "Is that why the lass is running now?"

And she was. He'd just caught her scent — woman, sex, temptation — drifting on the wind. He turned his head and saw her jump into a beat-up old truck. She gunned the engine and raced from the lot as if the devil himself were after her.

He was.

When you run, the beast likes to hunt.

"Are you certain it's her? We're not about to terrify some mortal, are we?" Liam pressed. "Though that certainly wouldn't be a first. They are fun when they're afraid. I like the way they smell then."

Alerac gunned his motorcycle. "She's mine." Absolute certainty.

He just had to make her remember that truth.

Remember him.

Damn vampires and witches and their curses. He'd been kept away from her for far too long.

"Then hurry and claim her," Liam advised him, voice roughening. "Because if you found her, the others won't be far behind."

No, they wouldn't. He'd gotten lucky. For once. A tip from a human who knew the score and who wanted to make an ally with the wolf pack.

He'd found "Jane" first. Finders fuckin' keepers.

The motorcycle shot away from the sheltering darkness.

He'd backed off earlier because others had been close by. She'd begged him to spare the humans, and he had. For her.

But he'd told her the truth. He wasn't letting her go. He couldn't.

He followed her red taillights and hoped that he'd be able to keep his beast in check a little longer. But he'd already waited two hundred years for her.

His control wasn't going to last forever. It might not even last until dawn.

It was just past midnight, when the darkness was at its thickest, and his motorcycle cut easily down the road. The woman who'd called herself Jane had ducked off the main streets and gone straight for the back alleys.

He wondered just where she was running to. *Is she running to someone?*

Jealousy was there, spiking in blood that was already overheated. But he couldn't stop the feelings. With her, he couldn't stop anything.

She braked her truck. Jumped out and ran inside a building—a boarded up, ramshackle building that looked pitch black.

He parked his own bike. Jane hadn't even glanced back before she'd dashed inside. She should have been smarter than that. Should have known that she was being stalked.

A vampire's instincts were normally much sharper.

Slowly, Alerac climbed from the motorcycle. He stared up at that building. It looked like it had been another bar, once upon a time. Now it was empty. Broken.

He inhaled. Caught her scent and—

A man's scent.

Human.

In that damn building.

With her.

His back teeth clenched as he headed for the door.

Another scent reached him in that moment. One that drove both the beast inside of him and the man that he was trying so desperately to be…wild.

Blood.

He didn't attempt to open the door.

He just kicked it down and raced inside.

CHAPTER TWO

When the door shattered and chunks of wood flew inside that old building, Alerac heard a man's sharp shout of surprise and pain.

He smiled. He'd be hearing that sound again.

He took a step forward, but then — then he was tackled. Something — someone — slammed right into him. Normally, he wouldn't have gone down, but the bastard had hit him with a silver-coated bat, one that burned like a bitch on impact, and *then* the guy had tackled him.

The man yelled, "Run, Jane!"

No, Jane wasn't running.

He grabbed that bat before the man could take another swing. Yanked it from the guy's hands and tossed it against the wall. Sure, his fingers blistered. Smoke rose from his palm. But he was long used to pain.

"Oh, damn," the man muttered, then he scrambled back.

Back to Jane? *No, you don't.*

Alerac was on his feet again. He rolled his shoulders back and lifted his head. His sunglasses had fallen. He didn't bother picking them back up.

He didn't have to hide here. They could see him for exactly what he was.

"What the hell is up with his eyes?" That was the man's shaking voice. The man—some blond fool who stood between Alerac and Jane.

"They glow," Alerac muttered because he knew the guy was talking about the shine that turned his eyes even brighter, "so that it will be the fuckin' better for me to see you." *And kill you.*

The guy leapt back, pulling Jane with him. Poor little Jane. So lost. She had a wall behind her. The fool in front of her.

And me, just waiting.

Then he realized that the blond fool wasn't bleeding. The blood wasn't his. Instead, the scent was coming from the discarded bag on the floor. A blood bag?

For Jane?

He'd thought the man was feeding Jane straight from his veins. Instead, he'd given her some kind of vampire take-out.

Alerac had heard talk that some vamps no longer took their sustenance directly from a live source. He just hadn't expected that to be the case with Jane. Her clan had always been particularly blood-thirsty. And they loved the rush of taking straight from prey.

"I thought you weren't a vampire," Alerac said as he advanced, crushing chunks of broken wood beneath his feet. His eyes were on Jane. In the darkness, he could see her perfectly.

Thanks to the eyes of the beast. The only eyes that he had.

Still staring straight at Jane, he asked, "So want to tell me why you need that blood?"

The male lunged for him.

Sighing, Alerac tossed the guy back against the nearest wall.

Humans. So weak. So easy to break.

He'd better not be her lover.

Because, if he was, the male might not get to live much longer.

He expected Jane to cower against that wall. Instead, her chin lifted. Her eyes—they seemed to grow brighter. Ah, so she was letting her vamp side out.

He could even see the faint edge of her white fangs, peeking out behind her plump, red lips.

"I don't know how you found out about me," she said, lifting her spine and squaring her shoulders. Like that made her look more intimidating. "But you won't hurt my friend, and you won't hurt me."

Her words had him pausing. "I'm not here to hurt you." Truth. Her friend? Debatable. Alerac thought he might enjoy hurting the male.

Her brows rose even as her gaze slowly slid over him. "Who are you?"

He didn't let his expression alter. "Alerac," he gritted out. "Alerac O'Neill."

The name seemed to mean nothing to her. A frown still pulling her brows low, she demanded, "*What* are you?"

His head tilted as he heard the roar of an engine. Several engines. Big vehicles. SUVs. Coming fast toward their location. His gaze shifted to the human on the floor. Then back to Jane. "I'm the man who is going to keep you alive."

Her laughter was sharp and disbelieving. "You're the only threat I see here!"

"I hear them coming for you." There wasn't a lot of time to waste. But he'd try to get her to leave willingly with him. If that didn't work...

She will still leave with me.

"The enemies coming didn't follow me. I didn't lead them to you." He wanted her to understand that. "And no one else followed you when you left that bar. I made sure of that."

She licked her lower lip. A nervous gesture.

One that made him *ache. It has been too long since I've been with her.*

A growl rose in his throat. "So if they didn't follow me...or you...someone else must have told them where you were." The *someone* who was now trying to crawl his way toward the door.

He wasn't escaping.

Alerac leapt over and grabbed the human. Alerac lifted him up and shoved the man against the wall. "She called you, didn't she?" Ah, yes, now he recognized the fellow. Dr. Heath Myers. Alerac had seen a grainy photo of the doctor before. Alerac's human informant had briefed Alerac about the man.

The man who'd found a lost woman walking on the edge of a swamp. A woman with no memory. No past. A woman who had a thirst for blood and who weakened in sunlight.

Not a lost woman, but a lost vampire.

"Jane told you I was at the bar, that I knew what she was," Alerac said.

The doctor didn't speak. He didn't need to. Alerac realized exactly what had happened.

Rage building, Alerac charged, "You realized you had to act fast, or you were about to lose your payday."

"Stop it!" Jane grabbed Alerac's arm and tried to yank him away from the doctor. Not happening. Even on his weakest day, he was far stronger than she could imagine. "You don't know what you're talking about! Heath is here to help me!"

No, he wasn't.

"Two minutes," Alerac told her. He kept his hold on the squirming doctor. "That's how long you have before the others get here."

She stared up at him with those big, blue, fuck-me eyes. "O-others?"

So many enemies. All eager to use her. "Come with me," he told her, "and I'll make sure you live."

She shook her head.

If that was the way she wanted to play it.

"I don't even know you, Alerac O'Neill!" She yanked harder on his arm. "But I know Heath. I trust him."

She shouldn't.

"He saved my life! Helped me to—to live in a world I don't know."

Then Alerac felt it. The hard, fast slice of a blade in his chest. A silver blade. There was no mistaking that familiar burn.

His gaze shot to the doctor. The man wasn't squirming any longer. He was smiling. "I know how to kill your kind," Heath whispered.

Silver. Right to the heart.

Normally, that was an effective method for killing a werewolf.

He backed away from the doctor.

Jane got a look at his chest and the knife protruding from it. She screamed.

Normally. Alerac's knees gave way. He sank to the floor. His fingers curled around the knife's handle.

Heath grabbed Jane's hand. "Let's go!"

If Jane left, she'd be dead.

But she wasn't running. She was staring at Alerac with horror filling her eyes.

"Jane, come *on!*" Heath jerked her toward the door.

Wrong move.

The guy had probably just bruised her.

Alerac slowly pulled the knife out of his chest as the smoke drifted from the wound. "You don't know anything about *my* kind," he said to the doctor. The knife hit the floor. He didn't need that weapon. Razor sharp claws burst from his fingertips. "But you will, human. I promise, *you will.*"

Heath dragged Jane through the broken door. She'd caught sight of Alerac's claws. And, judging by the fear flying across her face, she hadn't been prepared to see them.

The woman looked as if she'd never seen a werewolf's claws before.

Fuckin' Lorcan. He'd done this to her. Taken away her past. Destroyed her memories.

"Run, Jane, hurry!" Heath's shout.

Alerac followed them to the doorway. The sound of approaching engines could be heard clearly now. Those growls were too close. "Go with him," Alerac called, "and he'll turn on you."

Jane's breath panted out, but she pulled away from Heath. Whirled back to face Alerac.

"Trust me." He wanted her to come to him. To take that step. Willingly.

But Jane shook her head. "I don't know you."

Then she jumped into her truck. Heath was already inside, sitting next to the passenger door. Jane floored the vehicle. It lurched forward.

Heath glanced back. Flipped him the middle finger.

A low whistle came from the Alerac's right. "I guess we get to kill that human, huh?" Liam. Alerac had known that the wolf waited just outside the building. Liam hadn't attacked because Alerac had told him to stand down.

But now…that human…

"He's a dead man." Alerac lifted his hand to his chest. His heart hurt, but it would heal.

With his shift.

The shift that was already pulsing through him.

Jane wasn't getting away, and he wouldn't fight the men who thought to take her in human form.

No, for their crime, they'd face his beast.

And they'd all die.

***

"Turn left," Heath's words snapped out, and Jane automatically yanked the wheel to the left. The truck heaved, then jerked into the narrow gap between two buildings.

Her white-knuckled grip on that steering wheel never eased as Jane spared a fast glance for Heath. "Did you see his hands? And why was he *burning* when you hit him with the bat?"

"Because it was silver. And because he's a freaking werewolf."

A werewolf. "What?" She slammed on the brakes. The pick-up shuddered to a stop.

"Don't stop! Keep driving!" Heath glanced over his shoulder. "He's going to come after us. I heard that once a werewolf gets your scent, he doesn't lose it. He'll track us—now shove down that damn gas pedal!"

No, she wasn't moving. Wasn't going anywhere. "How do you even know about werewolves?"

Vampires were real. Okay, they *had* to be real. Because she was a vampire. But werewolves?

Her head was throbbing, the temples feeling like they were ready to burst.

"I know because after I found *you,* I did some checking." He was sweating. And she could see the pulse beating frantically along his throat. "I was trying to help you, Jane. That's all I've ever wanted, since the first moment I found you."

She stared at him as the truck's engine idled. Heath. Her only real friend in this messed up world. "You're the first thing I remember." She'd been walking, lost, slipping and falling her way through the swamp. The sun had been rising. She'd been so weak that her whole body shuddered.

I've got you.

He'd been there. Wrapping a blanket around her skin. Protecting her. Helping her

A doctor. Out in the swamp on his afternoon off from work. Poor guy. He'd probably never expected to find someone like her.

Someone who'd been starving. But not for food.

Blood.

He'd given her transfusion after transfusion in his small, isolated office. He'd realized she was…different.

Heath had protected her before she'd even realized that she needed protecting.

He'd even been the one to get her the job at Wylee's. She didn't have any paperwork, no Social Security card or driver's license—Jane had nothing. Hell, she'd even had to pick out her own name.

But Heath had called in some favors that Hannah owed him, and she'd been able to get paid under the table. *And been able to survive.*

"You trust me, don't you, Jane?" He asked her. Heath's hand rose. He brushed back the hair that had fallen over her left eye.

His hand was slightly cool. Not as hot as the—the werewolf's had been.

"Do you trust me?" Heath pushed.

She nodded. "I do." As soon as he'd realized what a freak of nature she truly was, Heath could have turned her over to the cops. To the government. But he hadn't. He'd said others would hurt her. That they had to find a way to protect her.

Hiding in plain sight had been that way.

He smiled. "Good. Now slam your foot down on that gas. You can't ever let that werewolf take you. Not ever, do you hear me, Jane? He's too dangerous."

She put her foot down on the gas.

"His name is Alerac O'Neill."

Yes, he'd told her that.

"He's a killer, and his prey of choice? The prey he takes down the most?" Heath swallowed. She heard the small click of sound easily in the truck's interior. "According to the stories I've heard, the guy always hunts vampires."

Like he was hunting her.

The truck lunged forward. But before she could make the next turn up ahead, two big SUVs shot out, and they blocked her path.

"They're here. Hell, yes," Heath muttered, sounding incredibly relieved.

She didn't exactly feel the same relief. "Who is 'they'? Tell me, *now*."

Alerac had told her that others were coming. He'd said that she needed to run from them.

"These guys can help you," Heath told her as he reached for his door. "I told them to meet us back there at the old bar. But *he* got there first."

Men were climbing out of those SUVs. She counted at least eight of them. They were big, tough-looking. All wore black. All also had fierce, hard expressions on their faces.

A shiver slid over her.

No weapons. They don't have weapons.

But one man was holding a duffel bag.

Before she could stop him, Heath jumped from the truck. He rushed toward those men. "She's here." He pointed back toward Jane as she sat, motionless, behind the staring wheel.

She forced herself to climb from the truck. Jane stared at those men as her stomach twisted. Were they human? It was strange that she should even have that question. Before that night, she'd thought that she was the only paranormal out there.

Before a werewolf came to her and changed the world around her.

Humans had to be close enough to hear those sounds. Those howls. The screams. The police would come. Right?

She stumbled back. Her hip hit the metal of her truck. *Get in. Get away.* She started to climb inside.

"Sorry, love, but you aren't leaving him again."

Another man was there—another man who'd moved too dang quietly. He grabbed her arms, pulled her close. Thanks to her enhanced senses, she could see him clearly in the darkness. She stared into his eyes. Golden. Angry. "He's killing for you. The least you can do is hang around and watch the blood." His smile was cruel. "I thought your kind liked the blood."

Her stomach was cramping. Nausea rising in her throat. No, she didn't like the blood. She hated it. The first time she'd actually tried to drink it, she'd vomited. She craved the blood and despised it at the same time.

Yes, she was screwed up. She knew it.

"Please," Jane whispered. "I just want to go home."

His eyelids flickered. The man before her was handsome, far too perfect, with even features. He had thick brown hair and angry eyes. Such incredibly angry eyes. His rage seemed completely directed at her. He scared her. They all did.

What was new?

She was a vampire. She should have been able to make others fear. She couldn't.

"Don't worry. He'll take you home."

The words sounded like a threat.

Probably because they were.

There were no more screams then. The silence penetrated her awareness. She looked back over her shoulder.

The wolves bent over their fallen prey. The vampires were dead. So much blood soaked the pavement.

And the black wolf, the biggest beast there, was stalking toward her. His green eyes glowed—glowed with that same startling intensity that she'd seen back at the old bar.

She shook her head.

The wolf began to shift. It wasn't some instant process. The fur seemed to melt from him. His bones snapped and reshaped. The paws on the ground became tanned hands. He rose slowly, lifting his head so that his shining eyes met hers.

Jane realized she'd forgotten to breathe.

He was naked. The muscles of his chest rippled. And as he continued to advance, her gaze dropped over him. She frowned when she saw the markings on his chest. A tattoo. One with intricate lines that covered the flesh right over his heart. Flesh that *should* have been sliced open from Heath's attack. Yet the flesh appeared completely healed.

Her gaze wanted to drop even more. She wouldn't let it. Instead, Jane made her eyes rise, and she held that glowing stare as he closed in on her.

Alerac stopped just in front of her. "You're welcome."

Her lips parted.

His head lowered toward hers. "That's twice that I've let you run. Don't try for a third time."

The words were a rumbled whisper of menace.

"You won't like the punishment I give if you flee from me again."

Then he was taking her arm. Her body brushed against his naked flesh. She gasped at the contact and tried to pull away.

Yeah, that wasn't happening. The wolf had a strength she'd never seen before.

Or, if she had, Jane didn't remember it.

But then, I don't remember anything before that swamp. Six months. That was as far back as her memory went.

Six short months.

"Don't run," he said softly.

Her gaze flew to the street. To the pile of bodies. She flinched.

Alerac's hold tightened on her. "I get that you don't remember, okay? Let me help you out.

That prick vampire? All of his men? They were here to get you, to force you to come back with them. They're working for a guy named Lorcan."

The name meant nothing to her.

"He's a master vampire," Alerac said in that deep, rumbling voice of his. "He's also a sadistic bastard who wants to make you suffer." He pulled in a deep breath. "I'm not about to let him get his hands on you again."

Again? That "again" part really scared her.

"You...protected me," Jane said softly. The bullets had hit Alerac. Her hand rose up, before she could even think about what she was doing, and she touched his chest. Her fingers slid over that heated skin.

He tensed beneath her. "Be careful."

"Your wounds are gone." No more blood. Nothing at all.

"The shift heals me." The words were clipped.

Her hand stilled on his chest. She stared up into his eyes.

And realized that his mouth was just inches from hers.

She also realized that her heart was thundering in fear, yes, but there was also more happening to her.

I want his mouth.

Just where in the sweet world had that thought come from?

His eyelids flickered. "I can give you everything that you want."

"Uh, just not here, mate," said the wolf with the angry eyes. That wolf also shared Liam's faint accent. "Local cops will be coming soon. They're on the way."

"I hear them, Liam," Alerac said. But he didn't move.

Jane frowned. She didn't hear any sirens. She was getting that their senses were a lot better than hers. Scary since Jane had already thought that her vision was pretty sharp. She could see well in the dark, could catch a scent from half a mile away, and she'd once heard a baby cry from four blocks down the road.

Just how good are their senses? Jane wasn't sure she wanted to find out.

"You don't know me." Alerac said this with certainty.

She nodded.

She didn't know him, and he'd just left a street corner full of blood behind him.

"I know you," he told her. There was something in those words, an intimacy, that had her body tensing.

"You've been found, little vampire," he murmured as his shining gaze held hers. No wonder he'd worn sunglasses in the bar. Those eyes would have scared all of the humans right out of the place. "Now that you've been found, you're going to find yourself in the middle of a war."

"I-I don't want a war." The other wolves were shifting back into the forms of men. Coming to stand around them. Glaring. They all seemed to hate her.

All but Alerac.

He looked at her as if — *as if he wants to devour me.*

She didn't want to be a snack for the big, bad wolf.

Alerac wasn't looking away from her. "Some will want to kill you. They'll want to torture you just to hear you beg."

This couldn't be happening. She wasn't in to the torture scene, not at all.

"Some will want to use you. A pawn with no fuckin' clue."

Her eyes narrowed. "What is it that you want?"

To use her? To torture her?

That glowing stare drifted over her face. "You. I'll keep you alive, but in return, I get *you.*"

Then she could finally hear the sirens, too. Like screams in the night.

"Live or die, your choice," the one he'd called Liam said. "Just choose fast."

She didn't want to die. What waited for someone like her on the other side? Jane was afraid to find out. If she was a vampire, did that mean she was some kind of abomination? "Live," she said, lifting her chin.

Alerac smiled. "Good, because you really didn't have a choice."

Her lashes flickered.

Liam tossed some clothing and shoes at Alerac. He dressed in an instant, then he was pulling her toward him. "Come on!"

"But my truck—"

"You don't need it. You don't need anything from your old life."

They were in front of a motorcycle. He climbed on. Motioned for her to jump on behind him.

She slid onto the bike.

"Wrap your arms around me."

Tentatively, her fingers settled around his shoulders.

"Come closer. Hold me tighter."

Her breath whispered out. She slid closer. Her breasts brushed his back. Her arms dropped. Her hands curled around his stomach.

The motorcycle growled to life, with a growl much like Alerac's own. Then they were lunging forward. Racing into the night.

She didn't look back at the bodies. She turned her face against his shoulder, and Jane tried to figure out how she was going to survive with the werewolf.

A werewolf who seemed particularly skilled at killing vampires.

***

That sure hadn't gone according to his damn plan.

Lorcan Teague stood in the shadows. The swirl of police lights flashed around the street, a sickening blue illumination that had his eyes narrowing. Humans were hurrying around the scene. Snapping pictures of the bodies. Looking for evidence. Roping everything off with their yellow police tape.

Vampires had attacked someone here.

They'd attacked the woman known as Jane Smith.

Only there should have been no such attack. He hadn't sent out the order for Jane to be taken in. What would have been the point? Jane was supposed to go off with the werewolf alpha.

In order for her blood to become stronger, she had to go with the beast.

He'd planned so carefully.

But it looked as if another player had entered the game. Someone who was screwing with his agenda.

That wouldn't be tolerated.

He turned away from the scene. He inhaled the scents in the night. The werewolves had fled one way.

Vamps...*my own kind*...had gone another.

His fangs stretched and burned in his mouth.

Someone was about to pay the price for betrayal. It would be a very, very high price indeed.

CHAPTER THREE

He drove until he could see the red streaks of dawn sweeping across the sky. Alerac didn't want to stop, he wanted to keep right on driving until he had Jane safe with him and back at his home. Where he could be certain no more vampires would attack her.

But the sun wasn't her friend. Hadn't been, since her twenty-fifth birthday. He should know. He'd been there that day. He'd covered her with his coat, trying to shield her from the light that burned her now.

The motorcycle braked near the rundown motel. They were still in Florida. Still miles to go before he felt secure enough.

But Liam was already hurrying inside. Securing the rooms for the group. Alerac knew that the humans at the motel thought they looked like a motorcycle gang. He'd heard the whispers when they'd all ridden up on their bikes.

The human staff members weren't completely wrong.

They were a gang, of sorts.

He turned off the bike. Jane was already
sliding off the seat, trying to get away from him.

He caught her hand, brushed his fingers over
her pulse. Enjoyed the way it sped beneath his
touch. "We'll stay here today." But he'd make
other arrangements soon. As long as Jane was
covered, safely away from that sunlight, his pack
could keep traveling. It would be easy enough to
acquire a van for their use.

Liam exited the motel's office and headed
back toward him. The werewolf tossed Alerac a
room key. He caught it easily, fisting his fingers
around it. "You'll stay with me," he told Jane. As
if there was another option. Hell, no, he didn't
trust any other wolf with her.

He didn't trust anyone else with her.

"Kent and Finn, you take the first watch,"
Liam ordered.

The two werewolves nodded. Their curious
gazes kept drifting to Jane.

Everyone in his pack had heard whispers
about her.

Now they all wanted to get close to the
legend.

As he advanced toward the motel, Alerac
kept Jane at his side. He sent a hard, determined,
back off glare to the others.

Jane didn't speak until they were inside the
small room. One bed. King-sized. Plenty of room
for them both.

The last time I was in bed with her…

Well, that time had ended in plenty of bloodshed.

And with her disappearance.

He slammed the door shut behind them. "You can rest here while the sun's high." Vampires were always at their weakest during the day. That part of the old story was true enough.

She had stopped in the middle of the room. Her eyes were on the bed.

How he'd like to strip her and *take* her on that bed.

The wolf inside was clawing at him, so desperate for the woman he'd been denied for far too long.

More than a lifetime. Hell, more than two lifetimes. Did she have any idea what he'd done for her?

He exhaled slowly. Forced his muscles to unclench.

If she knew, she'd probably be running. Screaming.

Instead, she turned slowly to face him. Her hair brushed across those glass-sharp cheekbones. "I don't like being in the dark."

His brows rose. "Most vamps do."

"That's not what I—" Jane began, frustration flashing across her face, but then she stopped. Seemed to catch herself. Or maybe she just thought better of yelling at him. She cleared her throat and said, "I don't know about the others." She tightened her hands into little fists. "I just know about me. Until tonight..." She gave a broken laugh. "I thought I was the only freak out there."

Anger hummed through him, and Alerac found himself crossing the room in quick strides. "You're not a freak." If anyone dared to call her that with him near...

Last mistake that person would make. Last.

Her smile was sad. "Everything I know about the world, I've pretty much learned from TV. I don't remember anything about my life until six months ago. I even had to teach myself to read and I-I'm still not very good at that." Shame whispered beneath that confession.

The instant she is free...I want her to forget. Lorcan's words drifted through Alerac's mind. The bastard. Alerac had thought he just meant that she would forget the pain of her imprisonment. All of those desperate years that she'd been trapped.

But Lorcan had taken every instant of her life away. Every memory.

"I need a witch."

Jane blinked at him. "Do what now?"

Not just any witch. He'd need a very powerful one. "You're under a spell."

She looked at him as if he were crazy. A growl worked in his throat. "I turned into a wolf right before your eyes. You're a vampire. Did you truly think nothing else out of the ordinary existed?" The shadows were full of monsters. She needed to realize that fact in order to keep surviving.

"Maybe I didn't want them to exist." A quiet confession.

What would he have to trade in order to the get the aid of a powerful witch? The price would be high. It always was. "We'll get your memory back."

Her head tilted as she stared up at him. "Do I want it back?"

No. There was no way that she could want to remember her imprisonment. *Maybe I can keep that part from her. Maybe I can get a witch who will pull up only memories before the day she traded her life for mine.*

"How do you know me? Were we…were we friends?" Before he could answer—and he didn't want to lie, not to her—Jane shook her head. "Heath told me that you tracked vampires. That you killed them."

True enough. He'd killed countless vampires over the centuries.

"Are you going to kill me?" Asked so softly as fear slid into her eyes.

"If I wanted you dead, I could have killed you behind Wylee's Bar." He could have killed the bouncers *and* her. Instead, he'd let the men live.

For her.

Jane swallowed.

"Your death isn't what I want."

"What do you want?"

"I already told you," and because he couldn't keep his hands off her, not for even another second, he pulled her against him. "*You.*"

When her lips parted in surprise, he took her mouth. The kiss should have been softer. She was delicate, almost broken, and he hated that. He wanted her strength back. Wanted her passion.

Yes, he should have used gentleness with her. Care. But he wasn't human, and easy wasn't the way of the beast.

His tongue thrust into her mouth as he lifted her up against him. So small. He took three steps, and he had her body pinned against the wall.

He would have gone straight for the bed, but he was trying — in his way — not to scare the hell out of her.

The wall seemed the safer alternative.

Maybe.

Her taste. Her fucking taste was incredible. The first time he'd kissed her — he still remembered that moment — he'd gotten a little drunk off her.

He was getting drunk right then.

She tasted of paradise, of every pleasure he'd ever had. Woman and temptation. Sweet wine.

Secrets in the dark.

His hands were wrapped around her waist. His fingers brushed just under her breasts. He wanted to lift up his hands. To touch her nipples. Pretty, pink nipples.

She wasn't kissing him back.

She had to feel the thick arousal pressing against her. The way he had her lifted up, there would be no missing it.

She wasn't kissing him back.

His mouth eased from hers, just for a moment. "Kiss me back." Growled words, and not what he'd wanted to say. He'd wanted to say…

Need me. Desire me. Crave me.

The way he craved her.

He put his mouth against hers once more. His tongue swept over her lips. Pushed into her mouth.

And her tongue — *yes!* — she kissed him back.

Her nipples tightened against his chest. Her hips arched toward him, and her nails sank into his shoulders.

He liked the sting of pain.

Liked her mouth moving on his even more.

She kissed him with a tentative hunger, as if just discovering her desire again. He would help her to yearn, to need. He would guide her, show her every fuckin' thing about his body.

About the passion they had together.

Her legs lifted. Wrapped around his hips.

He thrust against her, helpless. Dammit, he wanted *in.*

She was sucking his tongue. Giving a little moan in the back of her throat. His cock was so swollen he hurt, and the only relief would come from her. He'd thrust into her, drive as deep as he could go. Her body would remember him. She'd respond just as she had before. "Keira…"

She shoved against him.

Because it was *her,* he let her go. Alerac eased her to the floor, then he dropped his hold. He stared at her, breath heaving, desire like a red haze before him.

"Wh-what did you call me?" Her breath came as fast as his. Her eyes were wide, filled with passion—and fear.

"Keira." He said her name deliberately.

Her hands flattened on the wall behind her, as if she needed the support. "That's…me?"

"Yes." His Keira. She would be his again. Always. No one would take her from—

"No." A definite shake of her head. "Don't call me that, understand? I-I know you *think* you know me but…" Another fast shake of her head. "I don't know you. And I don't remember being *her.*"

But she was Keira. Lost, but finally found.

"I'm Jane." Her voice was husky. Arousing. "Jane Smith. That's the name I chose. The only name I know." She lifted one trembling hand from the wall. Touched her chest. "That's me, not K-Keira."

She was wrong.

"You and Keira…you were…lovers?"

"You and I were lovers." The words snapped from him.

She flinched.

And he remembered the way she'd run away with the human. The doctor. While Alerac had been bleeding, she'd fled with Heath. Their hands had locked. She'd gone to that rundown building *seeking* the doctor.

With her memories gone, had Keira turned to another? To that bastard?

His claws burst from his fingertips. *"Were you with him?"*

She jumped away from that wall. Moved so fast. Vampire fast. And in the next instant, she had half the room between them.

He tried to leash his beast, but the possessive fury filling him was too strong to fight. "Your doctor," he gritted out. "The man who *left* you during that vampire attack. Were you with him?"

Her eyes were wide. "If I say yes, what happens?"

Fuck, fuck, *fuck!*

He whirled for the door.

She grabbed him. Forced him back toward her. "I wasn't with him."

He couldn't see past the fury of the beast.

"I wasn't, okay? And even if I had been…"

His gaze fixed on her face.

"Why does it matter so much to you? I was here for six months." Her words broke at the end. "My face was splashed in the paper. I was on the news. A lost woman with no memory." She licked her lips. "No one came for me. I didn't matter to anyone."

Lie.

"You matter more than you know." But he couldn't talk to her any more. Couldn't stand there and inhale her scent. She'd wanted him when they kissed. He'd caught the sweet smell of her desire.

No, he couldn't stand there, not with his beast so close to the surface. That was why he'd turned for the door.

Why he had to leave.

To protect her, while he still could.

"Don't try to leave the room. My pack is guarding you, and they won't let you go." He pulled from her. Spun around and grabbed the door knob.

"Your eyes…"

That whisper stopped him.

"They always glow. The other wolves — after they transformed — the glow in their eyes faded."

He nearly smashed the door knob in that instant. "I'm not like the others." His glow never faded. It couldn't.

Lorcan had cut out his human eyes. It had taken a very long time for the beast to regenerate new eyes for him. When those eyes had finally come back…

Not the eyes of a man.

And they never would be.

Just as he would never be a man.

He yanked open the door. Then Alerac walked into the sun, leaving his vampire behind before he lost all control.

***

Tracking the traitorous vampires was easy enough. They'd left plenty of blood in their wake.

As the sun rose, Lorcan knew that those bastards would be seeking shelter. Unlike him, they weren't at full power during the light.

But they didn't know his secrets. He'd been trading in magic — and even in science — for centuries. He knew that he was destined to become the most powerful vampire to ever walk the earth.

Soon, with the right mix of blood coursing through his veins, he would be unstoppable.

Lorcan approached the house alone. He didn't need an army. He could fight this battle on his own.

When he reached the door, he knocked lightly.

And then some fool actually just swung the door open.

Lorcan smiled at him. Inhaled. A human. One who carried a familiar scent. *Jane.* Only that wasn't her real name. To him, she would always be Keira. "You've made a mistake," he said to the blond human.

The vampires in that house rushed toward him. Attacking with claws and fangs.

Lorcan shoved the human aside. He would deal with him very, very soon.

He slashed out with his own claws. Took the head of one vampire. Disemboweled another. Drained a third. The blood flowed and screams filled the air.

The human tried to run.

Foolish, foolish human.

Lorcan followed him outside and slammed the human back against a tree.

"Y-you should be weak," the human whimpered.

"Should I?"

"J-Jane was weak in the sun."

His eyes narrowed. "Who are you, human?" He lifted him up and rammed his head into the tree once more.

"D-doctor Heath Myers."

A doctor. Hmm. "Jane's doctor." The name was familiar to him. Because he'd had eyes on Jane. On those close to her.

I should have been watching this one more closely.

Lorcan dropped the human.

"You killed them all," Heath's voice was hoarse. He started to wretch on the ground.

A sigh broke from Lorcan. "You're about to join them. You aligned yourself with the wrong vampires."

Heath swiped his hand over his mouth. "I didn't even know I was aligning with vamps," he muttered. "Thought it was…someone else…until tonight."

Curious now, Lorcan bent next to the man. His eyes narrowed on the human's face. "Let's just see what you thought." And he sank his teeth into the man's throat while Heath Myers screamed.

If you wanted to look at a human's past, all a vamp had to do was take a bite.

***

Darkness. It was always the same when she slept. Jane instantly sank into a thick suffocating darkness.

She was trapped. Her wrists shackled. Her ankles bound. The darkness was complete and consuming.

She cried out, screaming again and again, but soon her voice was gone. Gasps were all that could escape from her throat.

Her voice was broken.

She was lost.

There was only the darkness.

Tears leaked down her cheeks. She knew that she'd been left in the darkness. Forgotten. There was no rescue. No hope.

There was nothing.

"Jane." The voice, it was new. Voices never entered her dreams.

Yet she heard a man's voice. Low. Rumbling. Demanding.

She tried to see the man in the darkness.

He's not there. A taunt, from within. She was alone. That was the way that she would always be.

"Jane, open your eyes."

She could feel him, touching her cheeks. As if he were wiping away tears. She knew that she cried. The darkness made her cry. No, it was the hopelessness that did that.

Slightly rough fingertips brushed her cheeks once more.

Why could she feel him, but not see him?

"*A rúnsearc*," his rumble continued, and the language—did she know it? *Yes.* It seemed familiar, just as his voice seemed familiar, but the memory was just out of reach.

As all memories were to her.

His hands moved to clasp her shoulders. "Wake for me. *Now.*"

If only she could just open her eyes for him. But it wasn't that easy to escape the darkness. Not once it had her in its greedy grasp. She hated to sleep. Fought it with every bit of strength that she had.

To her, the darkness was death.

No escape.

His mouth pressed to hers. The touch was electric, sending a sharp pulse of desire straight through her body. His lips brushed against hers, and his tongue slipped into her mouth.

She awakened with a gasp.

And he stole that breath, taking it away from her.

His mouth lingered for an instant. She didn't fight him, actually, Jane wanted to grab onto Alerac and hold him as tightly as she could.

He saved me from the dark.

But then he pulled back.

She realized that she was on the bed. That big, king-sized bed in the small motel room. He was curled over her, his hands now pressing into the mattress, caging her.

His gaze—would she ever grow used to that shining green gaze?—pinned her. "You were crying in your sleep."

And he'd seen her. When she was so weak. Humiliating. "Sorry." *If you don't want to see me cry, then don't watch me.* She held the words back, for now. Angering the big, bad slayer of vamps probably wasn't a good idea.

"What did you dream of?"

Jane shook her head.

"Did you remember?" Alerac pressed.

Jane had to laugh. "All I remember is darkness. Having a voice that can't scream because it's broken." She shoved that darkness from her mind, but she knew it would come back. It always did. "I dream of being forgotten." Exactly what had happened to her.

Six months. Her face flashed in the newspaper and on TV. *For six months.* But no family had come to claim her. No one had come to tell her that she mattered.

That she was loved.

Forgotten. Yes, that was exactly what she was.

Not surprising, really. Why search for a monster?

"You were never forgotten."

Her gaze flew to his.

The faint lines near his eyes had deepened. "I should have transported you during the day, while you slept but—but you seemed weak."

Right. Weak. Wonderful. Just what she wanted to be thought of by this tough, scary guy. Weak probably equaled prey in his eyes.

His gaze slid over her features. "I thought it would be best if you had a day of sleep. A day to prepare for what will come."

That sounded ominous. "What's coming?"

His stare turned away from her as he glanced toward the locked door. "Vampires will hunt us in the night, so we must take care."

She lifted her hand. Curled it around his chin. Forced him to look back and *see* her. "What's coming?"

Those too-bright eyes seemed to burn through her. "You tempt much when you touch me. The sheets smell of you. And though you might try to deny it…" He lifted the hand that had cradled his cheek. Brought it to his mouth. Kissed the palm. Lightly licked her.

Jane shivered.

"You want me," he said, sounding both satisfied and *hungry*. "And the scent of your desire drives me fuckin' crazy."

Her breath caught. "A werewolf's senses…"

"Are ten times better than a human's." Grim. He licked her palm again. Nipped lightly with his teeth.

The heat surging through her body had her heart pounding in a double-time beat.

"So I know exactly when you get wet for me," Alerac whispered. "You'll never be able to hide your desire from me."

He knew. Horror widened her eyes as they flew back to his.

"My pack is waiting outside."

The faint snarl of the motorcycle engines finally penetrated her awareness.

Oh, crap, if he could scent her desire...could they all?

Yes. The answer was right there on his face.

Her own face burned. Talk about humiliating.

But Alerac shook his head. "They know you're mine," he said simply. "None would dare speak ill to you."

His. "I'm not...yours, Alerac." They needed to be clear on that.

His hold tightened on her hand. "Wasn't that the deal?" He murmured. "Your safety, but in return, I have *you*."

A desperate deal. She hadn't even realized just what she'd been giving away.

Had she?

"You fear me."

"I'd be a fool not to." A werewolf with glowing eyes and razor sharp claws. Um, yes, a smart girl would fear him.

So would a dumb girl for that matter. So would any freaking one.

The sound of the snarling engines outside seemed to grow even louder.

"Fear can be a good thing. It will help keep you alive."

He wanted her afraid of him?

Alerac climbed from the bed. Looked even bigger. She swore the guy had grown while she slept.

Then she realized that the pillow beside her bore the impression of—of a head. The covers near her were rumpled. She jumped up from that bed. "You slept with me!" He'd stormed out. Done his angry wolf routine, then he'd come back and crawled in bed with her.

While she hadn't even realized he'd been there.

"I protected you." He'd already turned away.

"Protected me from what? The motel maid?" She rushed after him, but had to do a fast halt when he hurried out of the room. *What the hell, Alerac? You don't leave in the middle of an argument.* She yanked on her shoes, adjusted her sleep-wrinkled clothes, and followed fast. "You crawled into bed with me because—"

At least six werewolves were on their motorcycles. All of them were staring at her.

Jane clamped her mouth closed. *Jerk wolf.*

Alerac glanced back at her, and a faint smile lifted his lips. "You were saying, *a rúnsearc*?"

What she'd been saying would be finished — in private. But her eyes narrowed to slits. "What did you just call me?"

That faint smile faded. "It's an Irish expression. It means vampire."

Liam coughed. Or choked. Hard to tell for sure.

Alerac eased onto on his motorcycle. Darkness had fallen again, but the moon wasn't blocked by clouds tonight. It shone, high and heavy, though not quite full, in the sky above them.

All of the men were staring at her. Waiting.

"Has she fed?" Finally, that suspicious question came from Liam.

Her gaze cut to him. "*She* can tell you herself." Her fangs weren't even aching. She didn't need blood every day. "And the answer is, no. I haven't fed tonight. But don't worry, I'm not about to start biting anyone."

A murmur — an angry one — seemed to go through the pack.

"Wolves aren't on the vampire menu," Liam told her, but only after a quick glance at Alerac. "Or rather, for you, only one is."

And that one had lifted his hand toward her. He held that hand, palm open, toward her. "Come, Jane."

Like she had a choice. But she wasn't a dog to be called. So she held her ground a moment longer. *Get the point, wolf. I don't jump at your command.* "Where are we going?"

"My home." A pause. "Your home."

She didn't have a home.

Her chest began to ache. *Unwanted. Forgotten.*

"And maybe we'll find a damn witch along the way," Alerac added, voice darkening.

Jane wasn't so sure she wanted to find a witch. Was her past worth remembering?

Maybe it was time to find out. Alerac knew her, he held her secrets—so why didn't the guy just spill them? "Why are my own kind hunting me?"

His hand lowered. He kicked up the stand on the motorcycle. Then *he* came to her, easily controlling the bike as he circled around and advanced on her.

She had to hold back her smile. She'd wanted that. For him to be the one to make the move. *I'm not jumping for you.*

But when that big, snarling bike and the equally big wolf came to a stop right in front of her, Jane stiffened. *Yes, I'm afraid of him.*

Afraid, yet she could admit — she was also drawn to the wolf. She should be running away from him. But she wasn't moving.

"The vamps think you committed a crime against them."

She'd turned on the other vampires? *It just gets worse for me.*

"And some of them won't stop coming, not until — well, not until I make sure they're dead."

Wonderful. "I-I thought vampires already were dead. The *un*dead, right?" That was what she'd seen on TV. She'd made sure to watch every vampire movie that she could find, hoping that maybe she'd find some kind of secret message or insight into her own biology.

The movies hadn't been helpful. She didn't sparkle. She didn't serve the devil. She didn't attack children. She didn't do *any* of the things that those vamps had done.

Well, except she did drink blood. But only when she absolutely *had* to do so.

"Some folks do have to die, for a little while, in order to come back as vamps." Alerac gave a slow shake of his head. "That's not what happened to you. You never died. You were born as you are."

Born as a vampire? That hadn't been in the movies.

"That's why you have power to them. Why you're a threat and why they won't stop coming."

She still didn't understand.

"Your birthmark. The circle of gold that surrounds your pupils. Those are both signs that you are a pureblood. Not made from a bite, but born to be a vampire."

The little mark on her left palm seemed to burn.

"I'm telling you the truth. And you have to trust me."

Like trust was easy. Trusting a human was hard enough. Trusting a *werewolf?*

"Get on the bike," Alerac ordered with a curt nod. "With darkness, they'll be coming soon."

She looked beyond him. At the thin row of pine trees. At the darkness. Were the vampires already stalking her? "They all want me dead?" All of her kind? Surely there was at least one who wanted her alive. She had a family somewhere, didn't she?

He didn't answer.

Her gaze jumped back to him. "Alerac?"

"You saw them," he said, voice devoid of emotion. "They fired wooden bullets at you."

Bullets that he'd taken into his own body as he shielded her.

"If those bullets had hit your heart, you'd be dead."

He'd kept her alive before. Her own kind wanted her cold in the ground. But he...

She climbed on to the bike. Wrapped her arms around him. Held him tight.

After an instant, his body seemed to relax against hers.

"There's a helmet behind you," he murmured, the words drifting to her over the roar of the bike. "Vamps can die if they lose their heads, so, this time, be sure you wear it."

Oh, right. She hadn't even realized...

Her hands pulled away from him. Fumbled. She got the helmet on. Then she started to worry. "What about you?" Jane asked.

He glanced back at her. Those eyes...her shiver seemed to start on the inside and then push its way out.

"I'm not planning to lose my head."

Yeah, but—

The motorcycle lunged forward. Wind beat against her, and she held on to Alerac as tightly as she could.

The rest of the pack closed around them as they left the motel. The scream of the engines was soon all that she could hear. The miles passed, and the pavement vanished beneath them as the bikes moved faster and faster.

The vibration of the bike shook her whole body, beginning first in her legs, then slowly moving up. She pressed closer to Alerac as the vibration continued.

She didn't know what to make of the werewolf.

A werewolf. The knowledge wasn't so shocking now. How could it be? He was right. She was a vampire. Not like she could judge.

If Heath were right, and all Alerac wanted was to kill her — he could have done so plenty of times by this point.

But he hadn't. In fact, he hadn't hurt her at all.

He'd protected her. Taken bullets for her. Killed, for her.

Told me to wear a helmet so that I'd keep my head.

They'd been lovers once. This knowledge was there. It was obvious from the looks that he gave her. Jane knew there was no denying what she'd seen in his eyes — or the way he'd touched her.

When he'd whispered *Keira* to her, she'd realized just how intimately they must have been involved. His voice had burned with desire and a heavy possessiveness.

Whatever Alerac truly wanted from her, Jane didn't think it was about her death.

He might not want to kill her, but the vamps sure seemed to want her out of this world.

She wanted to know what crimes she'd committed against her own kind. Why they hunted her so fiercely.

During the six months when she'd felt abandoned because no one had come forward to claim her — well, maybe she should have been relieved. Because if the vamps had gotten to her before Alerac did, would she already be dead?

The bikes slid into another curve.

Jane frowned, trying to locate a road sign. She didn't know if they were in Alabama, Georgia, or even still in Florida.

Her arms were wrapped around his stomach. The guy's abs were as hard as a rock. His attention seemed totally on the road. Hell, the guy acted as if he didn't even realize she was clinging so desperately to him.

Jane started to ease her hold.

His right hand lifted and immediately curled around her thigh.

His fingers pressed into her.

The touch heated her. No, *he* heated her. The awareness that she had for him wasn't natural. She recognized that. Fear shouldn't be so tangled with desire, but it was.

She looked at him, and she feared.

She looked at him, and she wanted.

The vibration of that bike continued, making her body too hyperaware and sensitive. Her thighs were aching. And she could all too easily imagine those strong fingers of his sliding between her legs.

Her eyes squeezed shut. Her breath was coming too hard and heavy and her—her fangs were growing.

That wasn't supposed to happen.

She rarely fed.

Her fangs *shouldn't* be coming out. She'd worked hard to control them. She'd wanted to blend with the humans. Not freak them out.

But her fangs kept burning as they stretched in her mouth.

"St-stop," she managed to push the words out.

Because something was wrong.

He didn't slow.

"Stop!" She yelled to him. "You have to stop!" Because a hunger was building within her, one that was making her body shake.

A hunger for his blood.

She wanted to bite. To sink her fangs into him and taste the werewolf. And that was wrong. As wrong as the desire that kept stirring within her.

A desire to be taken by him—rough and wild and hard.

To be claimed by the man that she didn't even know.

And if he didn't let her off that motorcycle—right freaking then—she was going to give in to dark impulses and *bite* him.

So much for being all confident with Liam and saying that she wasn't looking for blood. All she could think about right then was getting a drink from Alerac. Sinking her teeth into him. Tasting him.

Heath told me never to take directly from a living human. He said I'd lose control. That I'd kill.

But Alerac wasn't human.

The motorcycle slowed. Finally. Yes! Before it had even come to a full stop, she jumped from the bike and tried to put some much needed distance between her and her companion.

"Jane!"

She stood on the side of a highway. Underneath the twisting branches of a heavy oak tree. Her right hand was over her mouth. She'd slapped it over her fangs, horrified, because they were fully extended.

He shoved down the kickstand and stalked toward her. "We can't stop. They're tracking us."

Yes, true. But she couldn't get on that bike with him. There was no way Jane could be that close to him without biting. "I need—"

A shot rang out. Even as it thundered, Jane saw Alerac lunge toward her. His body hit hers—but he hit her an instant too late. Pain spread through her upper chest.

She and Alerac slammed into the ground.

Her shirt was wet. She *hurt.*

Alerac's hands were on her. "Not your heart," he growled. Begged? "Not your heart…"

No, no, her heart was still racing frantically. The shooter had missed her heart, thanks to Alerac and his fast reflexes.

The bullet hadn't driven into her heart, but it had still penetrated deeply in her chest. And she was bleeding. So much blood pumped from her.

"Find them!" Alerac shouted as his head jerked up. "Kill them! Every last one."

CHAPTER FOUR

Her blood was on his hands. Again.

Her breath rasped out, and her eyes — so afraid — stared up at him.

Alerac had taken her into the woods. Gotten her protection while his men hunted.

"The bullet is still in you." It had to come out. She would keep bleeding — she wouldn't be able to heal — until he got it out of her.

"Then…get me to a doctor. A doctor can get it out!" Her words rushed out in a whisper.

Jaw clenching, he shook his head.

He could see every inch of her so perfectly in that darkness. His eyes were a gift and a curse. He could see the terror streaking across her face and the blood that soaked her shirt.

There was so much that she just didn't seem to understand about her kind. Softly, Alerac told her, "Vampires can die from blood loss."

He wouldn't let her die before him.

She shook her head. Her back was against an old oak tree. "Get me to a doctor, Alerac." Her voice hardened. "He'll stop the blood."

Yes, but that would give them another problem. "Human doctors can't find out what you are."

"H-Heath…he knows. He kept my secret…" Pain threaded through her voice.

Heath. Alerac planned to deal with that human. "He didn't keep any secret for you. He sold you out." His claws pushed from his fingertips, and, carefully, he sliced open the top of her shirt. "And other humans would do the same. They aren't going to protect a vamp."

Her hands came up and pushed against him. "Stop!"

He couldn't. "It has to come out."

Her eyes widened. There was so much fear in her gaze. "N-not here. You can't!"

Howls echoed around them as his pack tracked their prey. There were no more gunshots. Just those howls. The fools who'd tried to hurt Jane would be running.

Or they'd be dying.

"I'll get the bullet out, and then your body will heal." He tried to keep his voice calm. Hard, when he wanted to bellow his fury.

"Heal?" Jane whispered. "I need to be sewn up! Once I'm sewn up, I'll heal!"

That wasn't the way it worked for her. Alerac suspected that Heath had deliberately kept Jane in the dark about the extent of her vampire powers.

"Don't scream," he told her. The way she was bleeding…it was too much. He couldn't afford to waste any additional time.

He took a deep breath, inhaled the scent of her blood, and then his fingers slipped inside of her wound.

She gasped as her body tensed.

He had to use his claws. Fuck, he had to use his claws on *her* in order to get to that bullet.

I'm sorry, a rúnsearc.

He glanced up at her face. Saw a tear leak down her cheek.

But she wasn't making any sounds. Wasn't moving at all. She'd frozen against that tree, as he cut into her.

They will pay. They will beg for death.

He had the bullet. It was still intact. He pulled it from her, slowly, carefully.

Smoke curled around his fingertips.

As soon as his hand left her body, Jane's breath choked out.

He stared at the bullet for an instant, ignoring the slight burn in his fingers. Not wood.

Silver.

The shot hadn't been meant for Jane. You didn't shoot a vampire with silver.

He'd rushed to knock her out of the way because he'd thought that she was the intended target.

It was me.

Instead of saving her, he'd gotten her shot.

"W-when do I start to heal?" Her voice was weaker than it had been before.

He threw the bullet away. "It will start almost instantly now."

Footsteps thundered toward them.

He spun, surging up to his feet.

Liam stood there, a pair of jeans hanging low on his hips. "They're dead."

Good.

"There were two," Liam said, his gaze darting to the ground behind Alerac. To Jane. "Both vamps. I took them out."

Even after two centuries, they were still trying to take her away from him.

"We don't stop again," Alerac said, his hands clenching into fists. *Her blood is on me.* "Until we're home."

Liam nodded.

"Al-Alerac?"

Instantly, he turned back toward her.

"Wh-when do I start healing?" Jane asked again. Her voice was so faint, so lost.

And…and the bleeding hadn't stopped. If anything, it seemed to have gotten worse.

He fell to his knees beside her.

"That shouldn't be happening." Liam stood over him. "Uh, should it?"

No, *no.* "You drank blood last night." He'd seen the blood bag. She'd taken it —

Jane shook her head. "I told you I…hadn't fed…didn't get the chance…before you showed up."

Dammit. "How long has it been since you took blood?"

She swallowed. Licked her lips. "A few weeks. I don't—I don't drink much. I don't like—" She stopped.

"Doesn't matter what you like, princess," Liam muttered and even he sounded worried now. "It's about what will keep you alive."

Her gaze was on Alerac. "I feel so weak."

Because she was. She was bleeding out right in front of him. Dying, while he watched.

Hell, *no.*

Alerac put his wrist to her mouth. "Drink from me."

She tried to pull away. There was no place for her to go.

"Drink from me. You need fresh blood. It will heal—"

"You said I would heal when the bullet was gone." Her lashes swept down, hiding her gaze from him. "I can't…drink. Not straight from…anyone. H-Heath said…"

"Screw what Heath said!"

Her gaze flew back to him.

"You're a vampire. Drinking straight from a source is what you do." Okay, maybe that wasn't totally true, but he wasn't about to go into the finer points of vampire lifestyle while she bled out in front of him. She needed blood. She was going to get it.

"I-I can't…" Jane said, her words even weaker.

"If you don't drink," Liam cut in, his voice cold and hard, "then you'll die. The bleeding is too heavy. Vamps tend to bleed too much anyway. If it can't stop, then you'll die under that tree."

No, she wouldn't. If he had to force Jane to take his blood, then Alerac would do it. There was no way that he'd lose her.

Her laughter was bitter, broken. Too weak. "I can't…because I don't know…h-how!"

His heart slammed into his ribs.

"My f-fangs…they aren't out. They were…b-before. That was why I…stopped…" Her words were so low that, if it hadn't been for his enhanced hearing, Alerac might have missed them. "I-I can't—"

He had his own fangs. Fangs and claws. Alerac used the claws on his right hand to slice across his left wrist. Then, before she could argue with him, he put his wrist to her mouth. "Drink."

She didn't.

"Drink or die," Liam told her, edging ever closer.

Her lips trembled against his wrist, the movement soft like a butterfly's wings. Her mouth opened. She—

Tasted him.

It had been so long since she'd drank from him. Too fuckin' long.

Her tongue licked over his skin.

His cock stretched, ached. *Too long.*

How many nights had he dreamed of her? How many times had he woken, reaching for her? Always searching, but never finding her.

He had her now.

Her fangs pierced his skin.

He shuddered. A growl rumbled in his throat. Her fangs might not have been out moments before, but they were sure there now. She was drinking from him, taking him into her body.

It was more than just blood.

Life.

He wanted her. Wanted to thrust deep into her even as she drank from him.

Some mistakenly believed that a vampire's bite was about pain and degradation.

He'd believed that.

Until her.

Until he'd learned of the pleasure that a bite could bring. A release damn close to the one he had from sex. Pleasure that shook his body, that consumed.

"Enough." Liam's voice. Worried. Angry.

Because she had taken so much from him.

He wanted to give her more.

No, he wanted Liam gone, he wanted Jane naked, and he wanted to be the one biting.

She doesn't know what I've become. Soon enough, she would.

"Stop her, Alerac," Liam ordered fiercely. "*Stop her*."

He didn't. Alerac turned his head. Met Liam's gaze. "Wait for us by the motorcycles."

Liam didn't move.

Alerac held his gaze. "Wait for us."

The werewolf gave a jerky nod, then turned and stalked away.

When he was gone. Alerac looked stared back at Jane. Her lashes swept over her cheeks. Her hands had risen so that her fingers curled around his arm.

She was taking his blood, drinking it so eagerly when she'd been hesitant before.

He fuckin' *wanted* her.

Her lashes slowly lifted. There was a faint shine in her eyes, one that hadn't been there before. The power that was inside her, trying to come out.

Hell, yes.

Her gaze held his. Her tongue slid over his skin and—

Horror widened her eyes. She pushed his hand away from her mouth even as she leapt to her feet.

A very fast move. Her strength was back.

And her wound had closed.

He rose slowly, aware that his jeans were far too damn tight around his cock.

"I'm sorry!" She'd put her hands over her mouth — over those delicate fangs — and the words came out as a mumble.

He shook his head. "You shouldn't be sorry for what you are."

He'd once cursed what she was, and he was glad that she didn't have that memory.

Memory.

Alerac stiffened.

In the heat of the moment, he'd forgotten one of the most important parts of a vampire's power.

When a vampire drank blood, it wasn't just about getting a rush of strength. When a vampire drank blood straight from a victim, he or she also tapped into that person's memories.

Will she see my memories?

Jane didn't have memories of her own, and he wasn't sure that he wanted her to see what he'd done with his life. She already feared him enough.

Her hands slowly fell back to her sides. "I didn't mean to hurt you. I-I took too much."

"It takes more than that to weaken me." Did she hear the rough edge of desire in his words?

Her gaze drifted over him. Down, down, then her stare jumped right back up to hold his.

His smile was grim. "The bite just made me want you more."

She backed up a step. Rammed into that oak tree.

"Don't worry, *a rúnsearc*, I won't take you here."

Another quick step back. "You aren't taking me *anywhere*!" Jane fired at him.

Yes, he was. But there was a time and a place for everything. "Our enemies are growing closer. I want you at my home, where I know we have the advantage."

His wrist seemed to throb where she'd taken his blood. He could almost still feel her mouth on him.

It made him remember the first time that his vampiress's fangs had pierced his flesh. She'd been scared then. Scared but aroused.

"You looked the same way then," the words came from him, unplanned.

Jane stilled.

"You didn't mean to drink from me then, either, but your fangs came out." They'd been kissing. He'd had her naked in his arms. For vampires, physical lust and bloodlust were so tangled together. Her fangs had come out. He'd wanted her bite.

And, after she'd bitten him, then he'd wanted *everything* from her.

"What happened after I bit you?" Her voice was soft. Husky. Temptation in the dark.

He turned away from her. "We fucked."

A twig snapped behind him.

"Stop backing away," he muttered without looking over his shoulder. The woman was always pulling away from him. "We need to get on the bikes and get out of here."

Her footsteps didn't follow his. He squared his shoulders. Waited. "Jane…"

Then he heard the whisper of her footstep. One. Then another. She crept toward him.

"Thank you." Incredibly soft.

Now he did look back. Curiosity had always been a weakness of his.

"You saved my life." Her lips lifted in a small curve. "Twice now."

He'd also cost this woman her life. "Save your thanks. That's not what I want." But he found himself reaching for her hand. Pulling her with him. Keeping her by his side.

They broke from the trees. The others turned to look at them. They'd all know what he'd done.

Werewolves weren't supposed to offer themselves up as prey to vampires.

Jane wasn't any vampire.

Mine.

His stare swept the men. No one spoke. No one questioned him.

They knew better.

Alerac stalked toward his bike. The scent of Jane — her blood — followed him.

Jaw locking, he reached into his saddle-bag and pulled out an extra shirt for her.

Then, making sure he shielded her with his body, he ordered, "Take off your top."

Her jaw dropped.

He smiled. She was just so damn cute.

"The shirt and the bra."

She edged closer to him. "What?"

"The vamps will follow the scent of your blood. So we need to leave as much of that scent behind as we can." Or, even better, maybe they could use that scent to lead the vamps on a false trail.

Jane grabbed for the top he offered. "Then I'll go into the woods and change. I won't do some kind of peep show for your pack."

"They can't see you." Not with his body blocking hers. "And we need to *move.*" They'd lost too much time already. Granted, that was his fault. He'd been too taken with her. Apparently, he hadn't learned a damn thing from the mistakes of his past.

She stood on her toes. Glanced over his shoulder. "Make them all turn away."

Fine. "Turn the fuck away," he ordered.

He knew they would.

She clenched the cloth in her hands. "Now you turn away, too."

He lifted a brow.

"Turn. Away."

He turned. Crossed his arms over his chest. "I've seen you naked before."

Her clothing rustled. "You aren't seeing me naked now."

A challenge? His lips curved. "I will be."

Her breath caught. He heard the slight sound. His smile stretched.

"I-I'm done."

He glanced back at her. His shirt swallowed her, but at least the blood was gone.

"I tried to clean off my skin with my old top. A little blood is left, not much though."

He jumped onto the bike. "Finn," he called out. A wolf with dark red hair drove his motorcycle closer. "Take this to the east. Give 'em a trail to follow, then meet back up with us at base."

Finn took the material from him. Rode off without a word.

Alerac reeved the motorcycle. Jane took up a position behind him. She wrapped her arms around him.

"Closer." A growl.

She slid closer.

Much better.

"Be prepared for another attack!" Alerac called out. Those hunting them weren't going to stop.

Not until Alerac saw them all cold in the ground.

***

The two vampires had been ripped apart.

Breath heaving, rage nearly blinding him, Lorcan stared down at their remains.

They'd died too quickly. They should have *suffered*.

"Jane's still alive." The human's voice came from behind him.

Lorcan whirled toward him.

Heath frowned at him. "You okay?"

No, he wasn't. Some plans could come back and twist and —*bite you in the ass.*

"I don't want Jane dead." The words were clipped. "Alerac had better keep her alive."

Heath edged back a step. The glimpse into the human's mind had been very interesting. Traitors had been revealed. Secrets uncovered.

Lorcan wasn't the only one with enemies stalking him in the night. Alerac had his share, too.

Foolish wolf. When would he learn? *Trust no one in this world.*

Even your own blood would turn on you.

"Wh-what do you want me to do?" Heath asked him as he squared his shoulders. "I told you, I want to help Jane."

"Such a lie." Lorcan was tired of the lies. What did they matter? "You want immortality. Jane won't give it to you." He titled his head to the right as he studied the man. "I will."

Heath's eyes widened.

"You can be useful to me, doctor. You can help me get what I need. If you do, then I'll give you exactly what you have coming to you."

Heath nodded quickly.

The werewolves would attack instantly if they were confronted by a vampire. But if a human came calling…

Lorcan smiled. This human would definitely prove to be useful. And, when that usefulness was at an end, he would die.

***

Dawn was coming. Jane saw the faint streaks of gold and red across the sky. She tensed, her hands tightening around Alerac. "We need to stop!"

He didn't respond.

He'd heard her, hadn't he? With his shifter hearing, he must have.

But she still tried again, "We need to stop!"

The first time she'd gone out in the sunlight, Jane had been hit with a lethargy so strong that she'd almost keeled over. When day came, she just got *weak*. No other way to describe it. Her body wanted to shut down and curl in on itself. There was no way she could stay upright on that bike during the day.

The bike began to slow. They were nearing a rest area. A deserted looking place. He eased into the parking lot, and the other pack members fell in behind him.

"Vampires don't burn in the sunlight."

"I know that," she muttered. She'd discovered that TV myth just fine on her own.

He shut off the bike.

"It makes me…weak." A stark confession. She was sure that lethargy would hit her any moment. She needed a place to crash.

"You have my blood. You'll be stronger now." He seemed so certain. She wasn't.

Jane hopped off the bike. Took off her helmet. She started to walk toward the shelter of the rest area.

Alerac caught her hand in his. "I know more about vampires than you do."

He knew more about everything than she did, and that fact pissed her off. She was walking blindly, and she *hated* it.

"We're close to my home. Just a few more hours to go."

The sun was stretching higher into the sky with each moment that passed. The weakness hadn't started.

Yet.

"A few more hours in sunlight," she muttered as she tried to tug her hand from his. "I don't want that, okay? I don't want to fall off the bike. Don't want to slam into the pavement and have you drag the poor, beaten vampire away."

"That's not going to happen." A pause, then he said, "Trust me."

She stopped tugging her hand and stared up at him.

"It's okay to be afraid."

Good. Because she was shaking in her shoes.

"But my blood is in you now. Werewolf blood is very strong. It's going to protect you." He kept staring into her eyes. "*Trust me.*" Then he pulled her straight into the faint sunlight.

She expected the lethargy, the weakness to hit her.

It didn't.

"I told you, my blood protects you."

Her breath caught. The sunlight was warm on her skin, and she didn't feel the usual weakness. Not even a little.

His gaze seemed to see right into her soul. "You have nothing to fear from me."

In that instant, standing in the sunlight, strength still coursing through her, she almost believed him. But deep inside, a soft voice whispered…

He lies.

***

"Tell me about the man who took Jane."

Hannah Wylee frowned across the bar. The place should have been closed. It was long past dawn, and she should be at home, sleeping.

But just as she'd been ready to leave, *he'd* come in.

Tall. Muscled. With icy eyes that seemed to see right through her.

She didn't even remember when everyone else had left. Didn't remember how she'd wound up alone with him in that empty place.

"Jane," he repeated the name softly. "Where is she?"

Hannah shook her head. "I-I don't know." Jane had run off, left without a word. Damn inconvenience. Now she'd have to get another waitress. She'd tried to call Heath and ram into him about Jane. Talk about ungrateful. After all she'd done for the woman. But Heath had been dodging her.

Probably because he knew how pissed she was.

"Someone else was here, someone was after Jane." His voice seemed to pour into Hannah.

Her brow furrowed. She felt like they'd been talking about Jane for a long time, but she couldn't be sure.

"I don't want to hurt you, Hannah," he murmured. There was no accent in his voice. Just darkness. "But I will, if you don't tell me what I need to know."

His words should have terrified her, yet she found there was no room for terror. She felt frozen. No, she *was* frozen. Hannah couldn't make herself move.

And he was coming ever closer to her.

He lifted his hand. His fingers curled around her neck. "The last night that Jane was here, what happened?"

"A-a man came in." She remembered that. That guy had filled the doorway, catching her eyes. Big and rough—scary. "I think Jane ran from him."

Those fingers tightened on her throat. "What did his eyes look like?"

She frowned, searching her memory. "He...he had on glasses." Sunglasses, inside the bar. More memories pushed through her mind. "I sent my bouncers after him." No one messed with her staff.

"What happened to them?"

"The guy took 'em down." She'd had to fire them. What good were bouncers who couldn't control one guy?

His hold was heavy on her throat. "And did he hurt Jane?"

She shook her head, or tried to. "She left. Ran out the front. Alone." Hannah thought that was the truth. "I haven't seen her since."

He stared down at her.

She couldn't look away from him.

He sighed. "Hannah, I need to know the truth. Don't worry, it will only hurt for a moment."

He was beautiful. Gorgeous. The best-looking man she'd ever seen. And something was wrong with her. He'd done something to her, she knew he had. Because she wouldn't have told him so much about Jane. Wouldn't have shut herself in there alone with him.

What did he do?

She forced herself to speak. "Wh-what will hurt?"

"This."

She expected him to strangle her. But his head ducked toward her throat. Something sharp sliced across her jugular.

Hannah didn't even have the chance to scream.

***

It was cold. The air had grown increasingly chilled as they drove — drove up higher and higher into the mountains.

Alerac had given her a jacket that he'd taken from his saddle-bag. Leather. One that smelled of him. One that made her feel strangely comforted.

Just as he did.

She hadn't burned in the sunlight.

She hadn't even felt weak.

His blood? Yes, it had to be.

I drank from him. The knowledge should have horrified her. It didn't.

Up, up, they went, until it seemed that they were in the very clouds. Dark clouds that threatened a coming storm.

They'd stopped only to refuel. Kept driving and driving. It had been more than just a *few* hours.

And now…

Heavy gates swung shut behind them. Iron. Clanging closed.

Alerac turned off his motorcycle. "You're home."

Home.

She stared up at the heavy structure. This wasn't what she'd expected. Made of thick, white stones, the massive house seemed to spring right from the mountain. Glass windows looked out into the coming night. Bright lights shone from within.

Her werewolf lived…here?

The cold air chilled her lungs as she moved away from the bike. There were a few other houses, much smaller, nestled along the mountain. Homes for his pack members?

"You'll be safe here," he promised her.

She truly wanted to believe him.

But when she looked into his eyes, they were hot and hard. Hungry. For her.

They were on his turf, and he'd already told her exactly what he wanted. The price she had to pay for the safety he provided.

Could she pay that price?

He took her hand. Since she couldn't very well just stand there in the growing cold, she followed him. The other werewolves dispersed, heading toward the other houses. Then she and Alerac were inside.

The first thing that Jane noticed was the fire. It blazed in a massive fireplace. Her gaze slowly slid away from the flames, and Jane saw a winding staircase that led up to the higher levels of the house. It looked like there were at least two more floors up there.

"Your bedroom is at the top of the stairs."

She glanced at him. "*My* room?" Just to be clear.

"Our room," he corrected as he raised one brow.

So he was still holding to that.

The door swung open behind them. Jane turned so see Liam heading inside. "Doesn't look like we were followed, yet."

Alerac inclined his head. "They'll come calling soon enough. We'll be ready for them."

The fire wasn't chasing away the chill in her bones. "Why is it that they want me dead?" Betrayal, check. But it was time for her to get some specifics. If she was going to be hunted every minute, Jane figured that she deserved to know why.

"Rest." Alerac glanced toward the stairs. "Then you can—"

Screw resting. "Why don't I have any memories?"

He glanced back at Liam. "Call in the debts we have. See if you can find me a witch."

Again with the witch talk. That talk made her nervous, but she pushed on, "Why can't I remember anything? We're here, we're supposedly safe. Just *tell* me."

Liam hurried into another room. She thought he muttered something like "Good luck with that," on his way out.

Alerac waited until Liam was gone, then he put his hand to Jane's back and guided her a little closer to the fire. "You can't remember because you were made to forget." His eyes were on her. Blazing now—brighter than the flames in that fireplace, and his eyes fully showed a stark, desperate need. "The vampire clan leader, Lorcan Teague, wanted you to forget me, so he made a witch put you under a spell."

Her heart was pounding faster. Shaking her chest. Her fingers had a nervous tremble. "You said…I know we were lovers."

That need got even sharper. Jane caught her breath.

"We were." His eyes held her trapped. "But werewolves and vampires aren't supposed to mate. We're supposed to fight. To hate. To kill one another." His fingers skimmed over her cheek. "Not to fuck."

Okay, now the fire was a little too hot. Or maybe she was a little too hot. Jane edged back.

"We weren't supposed to be together," Alerac continued, and his fingers brushed back her hair. "And Lorcan wanted to make sure that when you were free, you didn't remember me."

His head bent.

She tensed.

His lips brushed over her throat.

A shiver slid over her. That shiver had nothing to do with nervousness and everything to do with desire. Her sex was suddenly aching. Her nipples were tight. When she'd taken his blood before, it had been as if a gate had broken open inside of her. She'd been flooded with emotion. Need.

Lust.

For him.

"The bastard thought I'd be long dead by the time you were free. That you wouldn't remember what he'd done." His voice roughened even more. "I showed him." Another sensual press of his lips along her throat.

Her knees were starting to feel funny. "Why would you be…long dead?"

His head lifted. "Werewolves aren't immortal."

She'd never get used to those glowing eyes. Eyes that saw *in* to her.

"You were locked away."

"Locked away?"

"I don't know where. I couldn't find you. I looked and I looked, but you were gone."

Her lips had turned desert dry. "For how long?"

She'd demanded the truth, but in that instant, Jane didn't think she wanted to hear—

"Two hundred years."

No, she definitely hadn't wanted to hear that truth.

CHAPTER FIVE

Jane was in his home. Where he could keep her safe.

He could hear the rush of the shower's water pounding down on her. After he'd told her that she'd been imprisoned for over two hundred years, he'd expected more questions. Instead, she'd turned and headed up the stairs without a word.

He'd followed her.

He felt like he was always fuckin' following her.

She won't get away again.

He stood before the closed bathroom door. Jane was inside. Naked.

He'd stripped off his own shirt. Now he wore only a pair of loose jeans that hung on his hips.

Did Jane realize just how delicate his control was? Probably not. She didn't seem to understand just how desperately his beast wanted her.

His wolf had been denied its mate for far too long.

He couldn't be denied any longer.

The water stopped.

Rustles. Whispers.

Move away. It would be wise to move away from the door. To give her some space, but…

The wolf within him wasn't letting him move. The man was at the end of his rope. Too hungry for her. Too desperate to reclaim what had been stolen from him.

No, he shouldn't have lived for two hundred years. But he hadn't been about to give up.

Sometimes, you didn't realize what you had until it was gone.

The door creaked open.

Jane stood there, clad only in her towel.

Once you realized just how valuable some things — some people — were, you'd fight even the devil to get them back.

For her, he'd fight anyone. Everyone.

Her gaze lifted to find his. "Alerac…"

He reached for her. Kissed her before she could speak again. He loved her taste. It drove him wild.

Her skin was soft beneath his hands. Still wet from the shower. He wanted to lick that skin. He wanted to lick every single inch of her body.

Mate.

He'd never claimed her as his mate before. He wouldn't make the same mistake again.

He lifted her up against him. Held her easily in his arms. She was so small and delicate. When they'd first met, and she'd still been more human than vampire, that delicacy had scared him.

She'd been too breakable.

He'd waited to take her then, so desperate for her to change and become a full vampire — so that he couldn't hurt her.

A werewolf's passion wasn't an easy thing. Rough. Wild. Savage.

After waiting for so long now, that savagery was just beneath his surface.

His claws wanted to come out. He wanted to snarl and howl and take.

But the man held onto control. Barely.

He carried her toward the bed. Put her on the heavy covers. Pulled back to stare down at her.

Did she want him? He inhaled, desperate to see —

"Why do I feel this way?" Her voice was a husky stroke right over his skin. "No matter what happened before, I shouldn't want you this badly."

Yes, you should. "There's nothing wrong with desire." Not a damn thing.

Her wet hair spread behind her on the bed. The towel was knotted between her breasts.

She stared up at him. Her eyes were so blue. As blue as the skies over Ireland, the home she'd once had. "I don't know you," she whispered.

You did. "Then get to know me." At first, he'd wanted her to get all of her memories back. But now, in truth, there were parts of their past that he never wanted her to remember. Selfish? Yeah, but it would be easier to forget those parts.

The betrayals. The lies.

He reached for her hand. Brought it to his lips. He kissed her knuckles and turned her hand over so that he could score his teeth over her palm.

Her breath hissed out.

"Your body knows me, and I know it." *That towel needs to come off.* He had to make this good for her, before the beast took over for him.

Too long.

"I've dreamed of you in this bed." A stark confession from him.

Jane shook her head. "I never have dreams. Only darkness."

When he'd lost his sight, she'd been the only light in his darkness.

He licked her palm. Then Alerac inhaled the tempting scent of her arousal. She wanted him. She feared him, but she wanted him.

He put her hand back on the bed. Let his fingers trail up the silken skin of her thighs.

"J-just so you know…" she told him, watching him with desire shadowing her eyes. "This isn't because I owe you for my life."

His fingers eased up a few more inches, pushing away that towel. "Then what is it about?"

She rasped out a quick breath. "Desire."

Oh, he was well acquainted with desire.

"It's not natural, the way I feel about you," she whispered. "I shouldn't want you this much."

Yes, she should. "Maybe your body just remembers what your mind can't."

"Don't…"

The one word had his head jerking up. If she was telling him to stop, to back away, he would.

For her, he'd do anything.

But then she said, "Don't hurt me."

She fuckin' broke his heart. The heart too many had tried to carve right out of his chest. The heart he'd given to her two centuries before.

"I won't." Then he was unknotting that towel. Peeling it away from her body. She was just as she'd been in his dreams. Those perfect, round breasts with their pink-tipped nipples. The soft curve of her stomach. The lush flare of her hips.

The temptation of her sex — soft and pink and waiting.

He bent his head and took a breast between his lips. Licking. Sucking. Tasting. The nipple was hard and tight and he loved the way she gasped and arched toward him.

He kept tasting her, sampling her, even as his fingers slid down her stomach and pushed between her legs.

She was wet for him.

Already.

Yes.

Her hands were on his back, her nails lightly raking over his skin. He'd wanted her touch for too long.

His eyes squeezed shut as he kissed his way down her stomach.

"Alerac?"

He kept kissing her. He'd taste the need she had for him. He'd make sure to give her pleasure before the beast broke free.

Her pleasure mattered. If he made it good enough for him, maybe she'd stay, once she learned the truth.

He'd seduced her to his side before.

Can I do it again?

His hands pushed her legs apart. Her scent — so good — was making him light-headed with raw need and lust. He stroked her with his fingers, learning the secrets of her sex once more. Her hips rose helplessly toward him.

Her body tightened.

He put his mouth on her. He damn well feasted.

She jerked beneath him. Tried to pull away.

"Alerac — it's too much!"

No, not even close.

He used his lips and his tongue and he worked that sweet flesh until he knew that her release was at hand. He could feel it approaching in the stiffness of her body, the gasps that broke from her mouth.

He pushed his finger into her. Licked the center of her need.

Jane came against his mouth.

The taste of her pleasure broke his control.

He surged back over her. When she reached for him, Alerac grabbed her wrists and pinned her hands to the bed. He could see the edge of her fangs peeking out behind her red lips. Her eyes were shining with pleasure.

Mine.

He drove into her, plunging as deep as he could go, lost to everything but her. The bed heaved beneath them. The slats groaned as he thrust. Faster. Harder.

A growl built in his throat. The wolf was pushing through his control, demanding that he mark the mate he'd lost so long ago.

He wanted to put his teeth on her, right there where her neck curved into her shoulder. The bite would claim her. Show all others that Jane belonged only to him.

And it would give him her blood. The powerful, intoxicating blood that had first addicted him.

His canines were burning in his mouth. Stretching. Sharpening. He parted his lips. Put his mouth right over that sweet spot. He sucked the flesh.

A choked scream came from Jane as she bucked beneath him. Another release. Pleasure that shuddered through her—through him.

Don't bite her. Not yet. Not. Yet.

He yanked his mouth away from her and erupted into the core of her body. The pleasure was more than he remembered. Stronger. Consuming. Obliterating all that had come before.

Linking them.

Bonding them.

His heartbeat thundered in his ears, a mad drumbeat that wouldn't slow. Sweat slickened his back as he slowly lifted his head.

He stared down at Jane, lost.

"Y-you're still doing it," she whispered, her words a husky tremble.

His brows lifted. His cock was in her body, sated, but...*I want more of her.* "Doing what?"

"L-looking at me...like you could devour me..."

He smiled. That was exactly what he wanted to do.

Alerac began to thrust again.

Her legs curled around his.

She met him.

The pleasure rose once more.

***

She didn't dream of darkness.

For the first time since she'd crawled out of that swamp, Jane dreamed of blood.

Rivers of blood, enough to choke her. To drown her.

She saw men in an old chamber, a room made of stone. A fire flickered in a hearth. Voices were shouting.

Don't kill him!

The voice that made that desperate plea…*that voice sounds like me.*

The chamber vanished. She never saw who was being killed there. Jane was too busy staring at a new scene.

A dungeon. Two men were chained to the walls. When their heads turned, she realized that they weren't men.

Vampires.

"You can't do this…" One hissed.

"Watch me," Alerac said and—

Wait, Alerac? In that instant, Jane realized that she was seeing these images from Alerac's point of view. She almost seemed to be inside of Alerac and looking out at the world from his eyes.

Even as Jane made that realization, the river of blood deepened. Alerac sank his teeth into the vampire's throat and he fed.

The vampire died moments later, horror and shock still on his face.

Then Alerac turned to the next vampire.

"Don't!" The vampire shouted, fear making his eyes flare wide. *"I wasn't there! I don't know where she is!"*

"Of course, you were there," Alerac's voice seemed to boom all around her. *"I saw you."*

His claws reached for the vampire.

That vision—that dream—vanished. Turned into another. More vampires. Being tortured by Alerac. Being drained by him. He took their blood. Liam was with him, watching his alpha. Smiling with a sick and cold grin as the vampires died.

"I'll find her," Alerac promised. *"Even if I have to kill every one of you."*

"No!" Jane jerked up in bed, the scream breaking from her lips.

Her heart drummed, shaking her chest, and the sheets were tangled around her naked body.

In the next instant, the bedroom door flew open. Alerac stood there, dressed in his jeans, nothing else. "Jane? What's happening?"

I saw you kill—you killed my kind.

She'd been told that Alerac was a master when it came to killing vampires. She'd just seen the master up close and personal on his kills.

He rushed toward her. His claws were out.

She flinched.

Alerac stilled. His eyes narrowed. Those bright eyes. Too bright. That gaze swept over her. Then his lips tightened. "Been dreaming, have you?"

She jumped from the bed. Wrapped the sheet around her body. She'd been moaning in that bed beneath him just hours before. Moaning beneath a man who killed so easily. "I don't dream."

He went back and closed the door behind him. Blocked that one wonderful exit. "No, I guess memories aren't dreams, are they?"

She could still *feel* him on her body. "M-memories?"

"When you took my blood, I knew it would happen." He shook his head. His claws vanished. "Just a matter of time. With my luck, I should've known the visions would come the first time you slept."

She just stared back at him.

His hands fisted. "Right. You don't *remember* that part, do you?"

"No," she gritted out. "I don't."

"When a vampire takes blood from live prey, the vamp can tap into that person's memories."

So she didn't have her own memories, but she had his?

"I'm not sure which highlights you saw," he said, and she was glad that he didn't try to come any closer to her. She wasn't sure what she would have done. "But I'm guessing from the scream that just shook this place, they weren't good ones, huh?"

She gazed into those glowing eyes. "Do you have good ones?"

His fisted hand rose and pressed over his chest. Right over that dark tattoo that covered his heart. "I do."

"I didn't see them."

"What did you see?"

"You." Her breath felt cold in her lungs. "Killing vampires."

He nodded. "I've done that." A long pause. "A lot."

"But you weren't just…killing them. You were—you were drinking from them."

All emotion left his face. "Saw that, did you?"

"Do werewolves do that?" She hated being so lost. "You drink from your prey?" She'd thought that blood-drinking was something that only vampires had to do for survival.

Alerac began walking toward her. She backed up, instinctively, and her shoulders pushed into the heavy wood of the bedroom's wall.

He kept coming. Stalking her. Closing in.

"No," the answer slowly growled from him. "Usually, we just kill our prey and move on. But I needed their blood."

"*Why?*"

His jaw was clenched tight. "*You.*"

Jane could only shake her head.

"You changed me. After you, I wasn't just a werewolf." He sounded angry, enraged—at her? "I had to feed from them. I didn't want their blood. I wanted—"

He broke off. She was pretty sure her heart had just jumped right into her throat. "You wanted my blood," Jane finished.

"I guess you addicted me." Still angry. "You *changed* me. Made me into something other than the wolf I'd always been. I stopped aging. I didn't die, and the hunger for the blood grew."

So—what? He was some cross between a vampire and a werewolf?

"It wasn't just about feeding." Those images were in her head, and Jane couldn't get them out. "You—you tortured them."

"Yes."

No denial. She'd hoped for one.

But he just stood there, watching her.

"Why?" Jane demanded.

"Because they deserved the pain that was coming to them. They were there that night. They *took* you. They trapped you."

"And you killed them."

A little shrug. "It's what I do."

He *terrified* her. "No one should speak of death so easily."

His eyes narrowed. "What did the vampires look like in your dreams?"

She wanted to put distance between them. To run.

I can still feel his touch on my skin.

"T-two were chained in a dungeon." That was what it had looked like. Just like a medieval dungeon that she'd seen on a history channel special once. "One was blond. The other had brown hair. You killed the blond first, and then — then you turned on the other one, even though he said…" She couldn't finish.

"Dunstan said that he didn't know where you were." He raked a hand through his tousled hair. "He lied. It was his ship that took you across the ocean. Your blood that I'd found still staining the floor of the vessel."

Nausea rolled in her stomach.

"He deserved exactly what he got." There was no remorse from Alerac. "They all did."

She shouldn't ask. She shouldn't, but she did. "How many?"

He stared back at her.

"How many vampires have you killed?"

Then he smiled at her. Lifted his hand. Stroked her cheek. "My Jane...I stopped counting long ago."

She knocked his hand away. Shoved *him* away. She'd thought that she could trust him. That he could help her.

But he was just as much of a monster as the creatures that had come after her. Killing. Not caring. Again and again.

"Jane." Anger beat in her name as he squared off against her. "You don't know what they did—"

She locked her arms around her body. *Escape.* It was all she could think of. "How long until you drink from me?" He'd said that her blood addicted him. That she was the one he truly wanted.

Now, too late, she realized it wasn't about physical love. Or even some kind of emotional attachment that had linked him to her across time. To him, her blood was power.

And he wanted as much power as he could get.

"I could have taken your blood when I took your body." Cold words. Brutal words.

True words.

"I didn't," he said.

No, he hadn't, but she remembered a moment when his teeth had edged over the curve of her shoulder. When she'd felt just a flash of pain.

Then he'd pulled back.

"You wanted to," she whispered.

One dark brow rose. "Are you going to pretend that you didn't want to taste me? Because I'll know that you're lying. I saw your fangs."

Fangs that were emerging, even then. She clamped her lips closed, horrified.

"It's what we are," he said simply, shrugging. "When we fight and when we fuck, the bloodlust rises within us."

She didn't want bloodlust. She just wanted — *I don't know! But it isn't this!*

"We can't fight nature."

She wanted to try. "You found me in Florida. Then you brought me here…because my blood makes you stronger?"

His eyelids flickered. "I brought you here to keep you safe."

She knew he was lying to her. Jane shook her head. "Try again."

Before he could speak, she heard someone calling his name. Then Liam was shoving open the bedroom door. The werewolf glanced at her — a fast sweep with his eyes that took in her sheet-clad body — then focused completely on Alerac. "We have company."

The way he said it, Jane knew he wasn't talking about the good kind of guest.

Alerac spun toward him.

"Ryan," Liam said flatly. "He must have heard that we have her."

Alerac marched for the door.

"Wait!" She hurried after him.

Alerac didn't slow.

So she grabbed him and made him stop. "Who is Ryan?"

Jane didn't like the look that Liam and Alerac shared.

"Who is Ryan?" Jane repeated.

"A vampire." It was Liam who spoke. "A very powerful, very angry vampire."

Great. "Someone else who wants me dead?" Maybe they should just make a line.

Alerac glanced down at her hand as it curled around his arm. "I have a…truce…of sorts with Ryan."

"A truce that will be ending," Liam muttered. "You know it's gonna be over."

Alerac nodded. "I will speak with him. Have the guards escort him to cabin on the ridge. I'll meet him there."

So he was just waltzing off to meet this Ryan guy? "I want to come with you."

"No." An immediate and hard denial. "If he sees you…" Alerac exhaled. "I'll have an even worse battle on my hands."

"Is he the one who has been trying to kill me?" The vampire who'd sent men after her? *Twice?*

"Lorcan has been hunting you. As for Ryan, I'll find out exactly what he wants." His focus shifted briefly to Jane's face. "He won't be a threat to you."

That wasn't the answer she'd wanted.

But it appeared to be all that she was getting.

Alerac left her, with Liam following right on his heels behind him. There were murmurs in the hallway. Jane put her ear to the door and heard—Alerac was putting guards on her! Men to make sure that she didn't leave the bedroom.

What. The. Hell.

She started searching for clothes. She yanked open the closet. She'd take something of Alerac's and make an outfit. Just like on that fashion show she liked to watch.

Except she didn't have to make anything work.

Because one side of that massive closet contained clothes. Women's clothes.

"What's happening?" Did the werewolf have another lover? Lovers? Her eyes narrowed as she yanked some clothes from the hangers. She jerked them on.

A perfect fit.

She glanced into the long mirror that waited at the end of the closet.

The shirt that she'd grabbed was the same blue as her eyes. The jeans hugged her hips and curled over her legs.

She found shoes next—shoes that were the exact size that she wore.

The tightness in Jane's gut grew worse.

Whirling, she rushed from the closet.

She didn't waste time heading for the door and the guards out there. Instead, Jane hurried toward the big window that looked out over the mountains. She put her hands on the window pane and stared down.

Alerac and Liam were walking beneath her. The glow from the moon illuminated them.

They're going to meet the one called Ryan.

A vampire.

Alerac killed vampires.

He can't kill this one. Because something had happened when Alerac mentioned Ryan's name.

An image had flashed in her mind. An image of a tall man, with pale skin and blond hair.

And her eyes.

She wanted to see this man—this vampire.

She wanted to make sure that he stayed alive.

Jane waited. Watched until Alerac vanished down a snaking path that led into the woods.

Then she opened the window. Three floors up.

A fall like that would kill a human.

Good thing she wasn't human.

She crawled through the window, clung to the side of the house for an instant, then she let go and just fell.

***

"Where is she?"

Alerac schooled his features as he faced off against Ryan McDonough.

It had been five years since he'd last seen the vampire. That night, they'd both been covered in blood. They'd gone for each other's throats.

He could have killed the vampire then. Alerac had been moments away from taking the man's head. But he'd stopped.

Because Ryan had *her* eyes.

"She's free, I know she is." Ryan's voice no longer held even the hint of an Irish accent. Like Alerac, he'd left their homeland long ago.

Left searching for what had been taken.

Alerac glanced over his shoulder. Liam was watching them with a guarded gaze. Liam had never trusted the vampire, and he'd sure never understood why Alerac let the guy keep living.

"I was at the bar in Miami. I talked to the woman who owned the place. She told me—"

"Talked?" Alerac interrupted slowly as he sauntered around the small cabin. "Or did you drink her?"

Ryan's lips thinned. "I needed the truth. I got it. Then I had to fly all the damn way up here to catch you—and you know I hate those damn planes." Then he moved in a fast lunge and grabbed Alerac's arms. *"Where is Keira?"*

Alerac's claws had burst free at the attack. Even as Ryan tightened his hold, Alerac had his claws at the vamp's throat. "I let you come onto *my* land."

"Because you have my sister!" There was no fear in Ryan's blue gaze. Only rage. "And I want her back."

Not happening. "You need to step back. Or else we're about to see if you're still as much of a bleeder as before."

Jaw locking, Ryan slowly released Alerac. But he didn't retreat. The vamp kept standing toe-to-toe with him. "I heard her cries in my mind. Over and over again, until they nearly drove me mad."

He'd always known that Ryan shared a deep connection with Keira. Twins. The only born vampire twins that Alerac knew of in this world.

He just hadn't realized exactly how deep that connection went for them.

"I knew the exact moment when she was free," Ryan's voice was low. "Because that's when her screams stopped."

Alerac swallowed. "If you were so tied to her, then why the hell couldn't you find her?"

Ryan shoved him across the room. Alerac slammed into the wall.

"I tried!" Ryan snarled.

Liam rushed at him.

Ryan's fist sent the wolf down.

"In my mind, all I saw was darkness. All I could hear was her screams. I searched..." Ryan stalked toward him. "Just as hard as you did. I never gave up on her."

The vamp's fangs were out.

Only fair, since Alerac had never lost his claws.

"You just found her first," Ryan continued. His lips twisted into a savage grin. "But you don't get to keep her. She's my blood. My clan. And I'm taking her home."

The hell he was.

"Home?" The word was barely human. It took all of the control Alerac possessed to keep the form of a man. "A crumbling castle in Ireland? One that even *you* haven't inhabited in a century? And don't damn well talk to me about her clan. It was her clan that turned on her. That let her be sentenced to that hell."

"For you!" Something seemed to break behind Ryan's eyes. He lunged at Alerac. Punching. Kicking. Clawing. "You destroyed everything!"

As the vampire's teeth came for his throat, Alerac realized that Ryan hadn't just come to the mountains in order to retrieve his sister.

The vamp had come to kill him.

Too bad for Ryan. He wasn't in the mood to die.

CHAPTER SIX

She followed the sound of snarls. Of growls. And the scent of blood.

Her steps were soundless as she slipped through the woods. She expected some of Alerac's pack to come at her, but they didn't. Maybe it was her lucky night. She'd eluded them easily enough.

Or maybe she'd just caught them unprepared because they hadn't been expecting her to do a header out of the window. Whatever.

Jane barely breathed as she approached the cabin on the ridge. A small cabin, its exterior dark. But…

The growls were coming from that place.

So was the scent of blood.

She eased toward the narrow window. Faint light shone from behind that glass, and when she leaned closer, pushing up on her tip toes, Jane saw —

Alerac. With his claws slicing toward the throat of a man with blond hair. A man with fangs. A man who turned his head at that exact moment.

The man's eyes—blue, bright—met hers.

"*Keira.*"

She could have sworn that she heard his whisper in her mind.

Alerac's claws were flying toward the man's throat.

"No!" Jane screamed and pounded on the window.

The glass shattered, flying inward.

"Let him go!" She'd cut her hands on the glass. Blood dripped from her fingers.

Alerac's head turned toward her. His eyes widened.

This scene—it was just like the scenes from her visions. Alerac, killing.

A river of blood that never stopped.

"Don't," she whispered. "Please."

Then hard hands grabbed her. She kicked back, landing a hard blow to someone's shin, but her captor didn't free her. He spun her around to face him.

She found herself staring at Liam's furious face. "You shouldn't be here!"

Screw that. It was her life. She wasn't going to be locked in any room while the werewolves decided her fate. She tried to break free. Liam didn't let her go.

Liam…

He'd been in those visions. He'd taken the blood from the vampires, too. He'd fed, just like Alerac had.

And Liam's eyes were already dropping to her throat.

No!

She slammed her head into his and punched him in the gut as hard as she could. He stumbled back, and she raced into the cabin.

Alerac stood frozen, with his claws less than an inch from the blond-haired man's throat.

"Don't kill him!" Jane yelled.

"Keira," the man whispered. The word almost sounded like a prayer.

The name still meant nothing to her.

But that man…his eyes…*he* mattered to her. She knew it, deep inside.

"Please," she took a cautious step toward Alerac. "Let him go."

The floor creaked behind her. Then Liam's arms wrapped around her once more. "No more head butts," he snapped into her right ear. "I think you broke my freakin' nose."

Alerac's gaze jerked to Liam's arms. Then to Jane's face. "Take Jane back to the main house," he ordered. "*Now.*"

The blond man broke free of Alerac's hold. His fangs flashed — definitely a vampire — as he backed into the far corner. He frowned at her. "Who's Jane?"

I am.

Liam tried to pull her toward the door. Jane dug in her heels and got ready to do more damage to the werewolf's nose.

"Let her go!" The sharp order came from the blond vampire. Then he was there, right in front of Jane. He'd moved so quickly. Vamp fast. And he wasn't waiting for Liam to follow his order. The vampire grabbed Liam's right arm. Broke it. Then he pulled Jane against his chest.

"You're alive." The vampire was trembling against her. His scent filled her nose. He smelled like the ocean. The scent reassured her.

He reassured her.

And she had no memory of him at all.

But she found her hands wanting to rise. Wanting to hold tight to him.

"She doesn't remember," Alerac said as the wood of the floor creaked beneath his approaching feet. "You know the spell that was put on her. She doesn't remember a damn thing, Ryan."

Ryan. She tilted her head back. Stared up at him.

"I think she remembers me," the one called Ryan murmured. "Don't you, Keira?"

There was blood on his mouth. She hadn't noticed it before. Her gaze dropped to that blood, then she looked over at Alerac.

His neck was bleeding.

The vampire had taken his blood. She'd thought that Alerac was the one attacking, but had he just been defending himself?

The vampires want you dead. Alerac had told her that before.

He'd also saved her life.

And in your visions, he killed vampires.

"She doesn't remember," Alerac said again, voice rougher.

Jane glanced back into Ryan's eyes, so like the ones that she saw when she looked into a mirror. "I don't remember you," she told him, almost hating to say the words.

Pain flashed over his handsome face. "But you remember *him?*" He threw a hard glare toward Alerac.

"She remembers *nothing.*" Alerac reached for her. His claws were out, but his hands were incredibly gentle as he pulled her away from Ryan. "Lorcan wanted her to be this way. The bastard thought he'd get to her first."

Ryan's eyes had hardened. "But you put him out of commission, didn't you? I heard that you killed five of his closest allies—"

"And I nearly took the bastard's head," Alerac finished. "I would've…if I hadn't thought that I needed to keep him alive."

Her own head was aching. The scent of blood—now she knew that it was Alerac's blood—that scent was making her hungry.

"I kept him alive because he was the only one left who knew where she was. He killed those who took her to be imprisoned long ago. I needed him." Disgust thickened Alerac's words. "But now I don't need him to live any longer."

He spoke of death so casually.

To him, it was casual.

Her fangs ached.

Ryan held out his hand. "It's time for us to go."

But Alerac pushed her behind his body. "She isn't going any place with you."

Uh, *she* was standing right there.

"I let you live because of your blood bond to her, but I haven't forgotten," Alerac said as he squared off against Ryan, "not for an instant, about what you did."

Her heart was pounding too fast.

"You let them take her," Alerac continued in a voice that sounded like thunder's rumble. "You didn't even try to stop them. Didn't try to help her."

She eased away from Alerac. Jane saw the fury on Ryan's face as he leaned toward the werewolf alpha.

"And she took your fucking punishment," Ryan fired right back at Alerac. "When she never even knew that you were just using her all along. Seducing her, to get the revenge and power that you wanted."

The fierce pounding in her chest seemed to slow then.

Alerac grabbed the vamp around the throat. Lifted him into the air. "You're done here. If I see you on my land again, you're dead." His gaze shot back to a watchful — and still bleeding — Liam. "I told you before…*get her out of here!*"

Liam took her arm. Jane jerked away from him. "I'm not going anywhere."

She was sick. So damn *sick* of being in the dark. "I want my memories back."

He'd said that he could get her a witch. If she was under a spell, a witch could break that spell, right? "I want my memories, *now.*"

"Careful what you ask for. You might be better off without them," Liam murmured.

That was her decision. Not his. Not Alerac's.

Alerac tossed Ryan toward the door. No, *through* the door. The wood broke and shattered at the impact. "Come here again," he said, "and brother or no brother, you're dead."

Ryan cast her one final look. He was just outside of the cabin and — and wolves were coming out from the darkness. They circled him.

The wolves just seemed to be waiting. Their sharp teeth glinted in the light.

"One word from me," Alerac told Ryan, the words low and vicious, "and they'll tear you apart."

Ryan straightened to his full height. "This isn't over, alpha."

"Yes, it is."

Ryan's gaze darted toward Jane.

Meet me at the stream. Two miles south. Before dawn. Before the sun rises.

She bit her lip to hold back the gasp that wanted to break free. She'd just heard Ryan's voice — *in her head.*

Don't trust the wolf. Or his pack. Traitors want your blood.

Ryan's lips never moved, but she heard every word clearly in her mind.

But then Ryan turned around. He walked right through that circle of wolves. Headed out with his head up and never looked back.

Get away from Alerac as soon as you can. You must meet me before dawn.

She watched Ryan until he vanished. Then she moved to hurry away from that cabin.

But Alerac caught her wrist. His fingers curled around the delicate bones.

She tilted up her chin. "You should have told me that I had a brother." The anger was there, growing and beating inside of her.

"He can't be trusted," Alerac said, voice deep. "He was there when you were imprisoned. He didn't *help* you."

Not caring for the audience that watched, Jane challenged, "And you did? Is that what you're saying?"

No, he wasn't saying anything. Not then.

"I can't trust him. I can't trust you. I can't trust Heath." Her breath rushed out. "It seems the only person I can trust is myself."

A hard shake of his head. "I told you that I'd keep you safe—"

"I'm not some possession." The fury was so strong that she was shaking. "I'm a person. It's not your job to *keep* me anything." She'd been afraid, and the fear had led her to this place, this mountain with him.

She should have known to be wary of the desire he stirred within her. But she'd just been so happy to actually be feeling something again. Something—anything other than fear.

He seduced you once.

And he was doing it again. She was so desperate for some security, desperate for someone to *want* her, that she'd given in before considering all of the risks.

"Let me go." Her voice was flat. Surprising, considering that she felt as if she were breaking apart on the inside.

He glanced at her hand. Swallowed.

Released her.

She moved away from him and maneuvered through the smashed remains of the cabin's door.

All of those wolves—they'd sure come out fast enough. She stared at them, suspicion pushing through her. "They were in the woods, weren't they? When I was coming here…"

"They have orders not to attack you." Alerac's curt voice. "Just to make sure that you're safe."

"Safe?" Her voice mocked the word as she glanced over her shoulder. "Or that I stay captive?" Her laugh was bitter. "I feel like a prisoner." She rubbed her arms. "It's a real familiar feeling." She started walking then, heading toward the path that would take her back to the main house. "I don't want to be followed any longer. Keep them back, Alerac!"

She could hear the footfalls from the wolves.

"Keep. Them. Back!"

She wanted to break and run. To head for that stream. But…not yet.

First she had to make sure that no one followed her. She stopped. Took a breath. Then looked back at the werewolf who seemed to be sinking his claws right into her heart. "It's your land, right? Surely I'm safe here. I can manage a walk back to the house all by myself."

He studied at her, his gaze unblinking.

Jane realized that she was holding her breath.

Then he inclined his head toward the wolves. "Go back to your other duties."

They turned. Eased away.

She started walking again.

One foot.

In front of the other.

She headed into the woods. Kept her pace slow. Alerac would still be able to hear her footsteps. She had to wait. Had to plan her moment just right.

When it was safe, then she'd go to her brother.

***

"We should have killed him years ago." Liam shook his head as his bones began to pop and stretch. The guy had to shift in order to heal his broken nose and his broken arm. "I told you again and again, the bastard deserves a good killing."

But Alerac had never been able to end Ryan McDonough's life. Because when he looked into Ryan's eyes all he could think about was how much she loved her brother.

Even though that same brother had turned his back on her.

Her screams stopped.

Keira and Ryan had always shared a special connection. He should have known that Ryan was linked to her, even during her imprisonment. But if Ryan had been able to touch her thoughts then, why hadn't he saved her? Why hadn't he freed Keira?

Liam howled as he took the form of the beast. The others were gone, the small clearing empty. As for Jane…

He couldn't hear the soft sound of her footsteps any longer.

He marched forward. She wanted a witch, and he'd given the order to acquire one. But now Alerac had to wonder if Jane truly needed those memories back. Her life before the imprisonment had been short, just twenty-five years of freedom. Then two hundred in hell. Why should she be forced to remember that imprisonment? Why couldn't they just go forward?

The wind shifted, blowing against his face. A storm was coming. He could smell it in the air.

He could also smell Jane's sweet scent. Only that scent wasn't coming from the north, as it should have been.

The south.

His muscles locked. He inhaled again. His senses were the sharpest in the pack.

He focused, trying to hear—

Racing footsteps. Heaving breaths.

Jane was running from him. Again. A-fuckin'-gain.

His hands fisted. She didn't trust him. She'd given him her body, but that hadn't been enough.

"Why?" The one word tore from him.

He didn't move, though every part of him wanted to rush after her.

But maybe it was time he stopped chasing her. Jane was right. She wasn't a possession. She was a person. And if he caged her, how was he any different than Lorcan?

Liam was shifting again behind him. Turning back into the form of a man. "Go…after her…" Liam managed.

"She's running to her brother." Obviously. The bond of blood. It was stronger than any bond he could forge with her. "It's time he told her the truth, anyway." No more fucking lies or secrets. He was tired of them.

"Kill…him…" A barely human demand from Liam.

But Alerac shook his head. He could admit—to himself—that killing Ryan was beyond him. He could never be the one to take her brother's life.

That was a sin that Jane would never forgive.

So he didn't follow her toward the south. He began to walk back to his cabin. The home he'd foolishly made for her.

A home that was empty.

Liam didn't follow him.

***

She ran frantically through the woods. Twigs snapped at her and scraped across her cheeks. She kept slipping in the dirt and on the roots, and Jane sure hoped that she was heading south.

Then she heard the faint rush of the stream. *Yes.* She burst from the bushes.

But Ryan wasn't there.

The moonlight fell on the water, making it shine and glisten, as it tumbled through the rocks.

She looked to the left. To the right. "Ryan?" Jane called out. He should have been there.

She hadn't heard his voice in her mind again. There was nothing in her mind but silence. Nothing around her but the rush of the stream.

The air was cold. The wind blew harder against her cheeks.

Jane knew she didn't have much time. Alerac would realize that she wasn't back at the cabin. He'd come after her.

A twig snapped behind her. Jane spun around.

No one was there.

Hunted.

The instinctive awareness was back.

She bent to the ground and wrapped her fingers around a thick, heavy tree limb that had fallen down.

A growl reached her ears. Her head jerked to the right, and Jane caught the flash of glowing eyes from the thick brush. Her breath rushed out. A wolf. Alerac had sent one of his men after her. So much for not having guards.

She started to lower the branch. "I didn't realize that—"

The wolf lunged at her. A big, muscled wolf, with golden eyes.

She'd seen those eyes before, only they had been in the face of a man.

Liam?

He hit her with his paws, and Jane fell to the ground. Her head slammed into one of the stones that lined the stream. The limb fell from her fingers.

The wolf put his mouth at her throat.

She heard more growls then. Other wolves were closing in on her. She counted at least three of them.

"S-stop!"

They edged ever closer.

Jane realized that the wolves weren't there to protect her. No, that wasn't their intent at all.

Then the wolf above her began to shift. His fur vanished from his body as his bones cracked and snapped. The brutal transformation lasted only for a moment, then Liam's handsome face was smiling down at her.

"You should have listened to Alerac. The fool truly did want to keep you safe."

He hadn't shifted completely. His claws were still at her throat. He brought his mouth close to her ear. His breath blew over her cheek. "He would have protected you. But me? I don't give a damn about your safety. It's your blood that I want."

It was her blood that he was about to take.

"No one's here to protect you, princess. It's time for you to bleed."

His head slid down to her throat. She felt the rasp of his teeth against her skin.

No one's here to protect you.

Yes, someone was there. "I'm here," she whispered, and Jane lifted her hands. Her own nails had lengthened, sharpened, and she drove them right at his face. When her claws raked over him, Liam screamed and leapt back.

In the next moment, she was on her feet.

A white wolf lunged at her. She caught his head in her hands. Jerked as hard as she could.

When the bones snapped that time, the wolf stopped howling instantly.

The white wolf's body fell to the ground. Began to shift.

Her breath sawed from her lungs.

Liam circled around her. Blood poured from the deep scratches on his face. But the crazy SOB was still smiling.

"I guess the lost vampire has some bite after all." He swiped away the blood that rained down his cheek. "But you're still on your own. Even a vamp at full power couldn't take us all out."

She grabbed for the limb she'd dropped before. "Let's just see about that." Her words didn't tremble. Her knees did.

"Yes," he whispered as his face hardened. "Let's see." Then he motioned with his right hand, and two wolves leapt toward her.

***

Alerac froze when he heard the howl. It died away almost immediately, but the sound seemed to echo in his mind.

He turned to the right. Stared into the night. *Jane.*

He'd thought to let her go. But—

He took off at a run, and when he jumped over a fallen tree, his body shifted into the form of a beast.

***

She'd knocked one wolf back, snapping the limb in two when she swung it into the beast's head. The other wolf struck out with his claws. Those claws sliced their way down her leg.

Screaming, she rushed to the other side of the stream. Where was some damn silver when she needed it? Her fumbling fingers grabbed a heavy rock. She threw it at the charging wolf.

It smashed right into his head.

The wolf hit the ground.

Three down, temporarily anyway.

That just left her and — Liam.

He was laughing. Laughing and walking across that stream. "I forgot," he murmured as the laughter slowly faded. "You fed on Alerac recently. That would explain the rush of strength."

He was about to feel her rush of strength. Where the hell was another heavy stone?

Right…*there.*

She leapt forward and tried to grab it.

But Liam grabbed her first.

He caught her wrist in tight grip. "Your brother broke my arm." He shook his head. "Consider this payback." He snapped her wrist.

Pain surged through her. She shoved against him, but he wasn't letting go. Not this time.

"Alerac got to you first. He found you first in Ireland. Got you to spread your legs and offer your neck. *He* took the power that should have been mine."

His left hand fisted in her hair.

"Now I get to taste the blood with all the power. I get the bond that he wanted so very badly."

She kneed him in the groin. Punched. Twisted. He didn't let her go.

"I get your power, and then I'll get the pack. They'll all follow *me.*"

Her feet kicked against his, and Liam stumbled. They crashed right back down, only this time, they landed in the stream. The water soaked them.

His claws rose. Scraped down her cheek. "It's a good thing that your kind heals so easily."

Wait, what—

His claws sliced over her throat. Blood pulsed from her. The water from the stream— such cold water—covered her.

His mouth lowered to her throat. He licked her, taking her blood. "First claws," he whispered. "Then I get to bite."

"*Jane!*"

Alerac's roar broke the night. That fierce cry was the most beautiful sound that she'd ever heard. He was coming for her.

He'd realize what Liam was doing. She opened her mouth to scream for him.

But Liam sank his teeth into her throat. Pain engulfed her.

Then—then it started to thunder. No, not thunder.

Gunshots.

Liam's mouth tore from her neck, and his body fell away from hers.

She crawled away from him. Her hand went to her throat as she tried to stop the blood from flowing.

"Hurry, Keira! Hurry!" Ryan's desperate voice.

She looked to the left. He was there, at the edge of the woods, and he still had a gun in his hands.

Jane cast one fast glance at Liam. Smoke rose from the bullet holes in his chest. His eyes were closed.

Was he dead?

Liam's eyes opened.

No, not dead. Jane jumped to her feet and ran toward Ryan. He lifted the gun higher. Seemed to aim right at her.

She ducked.

He fired.

A groan sounded from behind her.

Ryan opened his left hand to her. She grabbed it, holding it like the lifeline that it was.

He pulled her close against him. "We have to get out of here," he whispered.

Great plan. Fabulous plan. Only…

She was bleeding so much from her throat. She couldn't speak. And she felt too weak.

He turned. Rushed back into the brush. She tried to follow him, but after three steps, she fell flat on her face.

"Keira!"

Hands lifted her up. She was tossed over a shoulder. Then she didn't see anything else.

But she heard something…a long, low howl that sent a shiver of fear chasing her into the darkness.

***

When he broke from the trees, Alerac's gaze went straight to the stream. To the stream that smelled of Jane's blood.

But Jane wasn't there. Three wolves were. Wolves from *his* pack. They were hurt, one was shuddering.

Yet, as soon as they saw him, they attacked. *What. The. Hell.*

They came in hard and fast—and they came in for the kill.

But Alerac wasn't the pack alpha for nothing. Soon it was their blood flowing into the stream. Their bodies hitting the ground.

They died in mere moments.

And he howled into the night, lost, betrayed.

His gaze swept the scene. Seeing so much. The tracks of a man, but the scent of a vampire.

The tracks of another wolf, heading away from the stream. Heading back up the mountain. That wolf's scent was familiar, and the sting of betrayal burned ever deeper.

Why didn't I see…?

The rage built in him, but Alerac held tight to his control. He left the broken bodies behind him.

In the form of the wolf, he inhaled deeply, pulling in all the scents — those both familiar and foreign to him. He locked onto the one scent that mattered. The *only* one that did.

The scent of Jane's blood.

He'd been willing to let her leave him.

He wasn't willing to let her die.

The paws of the beast flew across the ground. When he crossed the stream, he sent the bloody water churning and splashing around him. The others scents there — he took note of them.

Jane was his priority. Finding her.

Punishment. Justice. Payback. All of that would come. It would fuckin' *come.*

***

Liam raced deeper into the woods. No, no, *no.* Jane shouldn't have escaped. Her blood was in his mouth. Sweet and rich and powerful. Everything that he'd ever dreamed.

But she was gone.

Her bastard brother.

He'd told Alerac to kill the fool. Over and over, he'd given him that order.

But Alerac didn't take orders from anyone.

I'm the lackey who jumps at his command.

No more. Jane was his ticket to power. He'd known that truth for years. She'd been the one to amp up Alerac's strength. *She can give me the same boost.* As soon as Jane had been located, Liam had known that he would have to take her from the alpha.

He'd even hired those vamps to try and take her in Florida. Those men hadn't been working for Lorcan. They'd been on Liam's payroll. Both attacks had come by Liam's order.

He'd encountered plenty of vampires over the years. He'd drained most of them. But some, a few that he'd thought would prove valuable, Liam had let some of them keep living. They owed him, and he'd been collecting on those debts. Sending out those vamps on his blood mission.

He'd been the one to connect Heath and Jane. Heath had been working under his orders the whole time. Studying Jane's blood, trying to determine the source of her power—and of Alerac's.

But when Liam had realized that Alerac was going down to Miami to claim Jane, he'd sent his vamps to collect her. He'd known that his time to experiment had run out. He'd needed to make his move.

Only those vamps had *failed.*

But Alerac hadn't realized Liam was his enemy. Alerac was too focused on Lorcan. Always Lorcan.

Hell, Lorcan wasn't even in the game. As far as Liam knew, the bastard wasn't in the country.

Liam had tried to be careful. He hadn't wanted to battle directly against Alerac, not until he'd taken plenty of Jane's blood to boost him.

But his plans had changed. Alerac kept defeating every enemy that Liam had thrown at him.

Tonight, when Jane had gone off on her own, it had been his best chance.

I took that chance.

Now Alerac would know that he had a traitor—*traitors*—in his pack. Alerac would come for him.

His chest heaved. His claws cut into the tree near him as fury pumped through his gut.

Let him come. He knew Alerac's secrets. Every bloody one of them. And he'd use those secrets.

He'd take out the alpha.

He'd rule the pack.

Alerac would die.

CHAPTER SEVEN

"Hold on, Keira! Just hold on!"

The words sank through the veil of darkness that surrounded her. She groaned and tried to open her eyes.

But then her face slammed into something hard. Wait, was that a man's back?

Her body was bobbing, jerking, because she was flung over someone's shoulder. And that someone was running fast.

"I'll get you out of here," the guy was promising her.

Ryan.

The vamp who was supposed to be her brother.

"I have a car waiting on the other side of the mountain. I'll get you there, get you some blood, and you'll be fine."

She didn't feel fine.

She shoved herself up so she could stop staring at his back. Instead, she looked into the woods that they were fleeing through.

Glowing eyes stared back at her.

"Alerac," she whispered.

"He won't find us!" Ryan said, breath panting. He was running incredibly fast.

Just not fast enough.

He's already found us.

Alerac was in wolf form, and he was charging right for them.

Part of her, deep inside, was glad to see him.

"Alerac," she managed to say again, trying to warn Ryan.

Ryan just ran faster.

Until he heard the growls. Growls that were now far too close. While vamps could move fast, apparently Alerac was faster.

That's what happens when you're an amped up werewolf/vamp combo.

Ryan spun to face Alerac, but her brother didn't loosen his hold on her. "Stay back!"

Alerac didn't. He just charged right at Ryan. He hit with an impact that sent Ryan—and Jane—falling to the ground.

"Keira!" Ryan tried to grab for her once more.

But Alerac put himself between them. A big, fierce beast. His body vibrated with fury.

So did hers. Fury and pain and fear. A terrible combination.

"We…have to leave…" She forced the words out. Her neck still throbbed. Burned. Blood soaked her. Was she healing yet? She couldn't tell. It didn't *feel* like she was healing, but maybe the blood loss had just made her weak. Too weak to tell when her throat closed up.

Alerac growled again.

Ryan was back on his feet. "If you can't have her, then she has to die, is that it?" Ryan yelled.

Alerac didn't move.

"You sent your men after her. You let them tear into her because she wanted to leave you." Ryan glared at the wolf. "She doesn't remember her past, fine, but that doesn't mean she's your damn prisoner! She didn't escape one hell to venture into another!"

No. Jane pushed up to her feet. She wasn't in hell with Alerac. Alerac hadn't sent Liam to attack her. Alerac didn't even know that his men were betraying him.

"Let. Her. Go," Ryan demanded. "Haven't you hurt her enough already? She was punished *for you.* That time in prison should have been *your* time. She traded her life for yours once. Just *let her go.*"

She thought Alerac would attack him.

But…

There was no attack.

Alerac looked back at her. No more growls. No howls.

He stared at her, and the shift swept over him. Beast became man, and then it was Alerac who was on the ground before her. He rose slowly, still never taking his eyes from her.

Then Alerac walked toward her, naked and strong, with eyes that were swirling with emotion. "I didn't send them."

She nodded. "I know." Her voice was a rasp.

His gaze fell to her throat.

It was sure easy to read the emotion he felt then—rage flared in his gaze. "Consider Liam dead."

So easily? Liam had been with Alerac for so long, but he'd go after the wolf now? For her?

"You need blood," Alerac murmured. He took another step toward her.

Only to be wrenched back by Ryan. "What she needs is to get away from you!"

She took your punishment.

Alerac's jaw clenched, and he gritted out, "My blood will make her stronger. She's *hurt!*"

But now Ryan was the one standing between her and Alerac. "You just want to strengthen the bond between the two of you. A bond you manipulated from the very beginning! Keira should have never been with you!" He jabbed his finger into Alerac's chest. "Do you think I don't know the truth? Lorcan wasn't the only one using a witch in those days. I know what you did!"

Her hand lifted. Touched her throat. The wound hadn't closed yet.

Her fangs were out because hunger cut through her.

Alerac.

"You used magic in order to get to Keira," Ryan charged. "She turned on her family because you tricked her! You're still tricking her. She needs to learn the truth about her past!"

"S-screw the past," she whispered.

And both men gaped at her.

Did it look like the past mattered right then? "I'm *dying* here." The words barely could escape because of the damage to her throat.

Ryan's mouth dropped. "Keira, my blood—"

Alerac tossed her brother head-first into the nearest tree. "It's *Jane.* And I'm here." He caught her chin in his hands. He titled his head, offering his neck to her. "Take from me."

Jane didn't need to hear a second offer. Her teeth sank into his throat. She was so afraid of hurting him—the way that Liam had hurt her—and tears leaked down her cheeks at the thought of causing him pain.

As she stood there, her teeth in his neck, his body against hers, his arms came up. Wrapped around her. Pulled her close.

Thunder rolled across the sky. Rain began to fall on them, hitting softly first, then harder, washing away the blood on her. Soaking her clothes.

"Drain him, Keira!" That was Ryan. Annoying her. "It's what he deserves."

No, she wasn't sure what Alerac deserved, but she didn't think it was death.

Her tongue lightly licked over his skin. She loved his taste.

She also loved the power of his blood. Just a few sips and she wasn't weak, not any longer. Her body seemed to pulse with energy and life.

And lust had heated her.

Not lust for his blood.

For him.

She pulled her mouth from his neck. Alerac's head lifted. Raindrops clung to his lashes as he peered down at her. "I didn't send them after you."

An understanding sank into her, one that left her feeling lost. "You weren't coming after me at all, were you?" He'd known that she'd run. Of course, he'd known. Mr. Super Senses.

He shook his head. "Not until I heard the howls."

The howls had come when the werewolves attacked her. "What happened to them?" Jane whispered.

"Three are dead." The lines near his mouth deepened. "The fourth *will* be."

The dangerous intent in his voice made goosebumps rise on her arms.

"All right, she's strong again. Not get away from her." Ryan's words rapped out. "It's time for us to leave, Keira."

"Jane," Alerac corrected in a hard, tight voice. "She wants to be called Jane now."

Ryan blinked. "What? Jane isn't her name. It's—"

Her shoulders straightened. "I don't know Keira. I don't...I don't know you."

He blanched.

"I'm Jane, and—" Oh, crap, this could be one huge mistake. But with his blood strengthening her, with his arms still around her, with Alerac's eyes on her in that intense look that seemed to be breaking her heart, she could only say, "And I'm not leaving him."

She couldn't tell who was more surprised by her announcement.

Ryan.

Or Alerac.

Or, hell, *maybe even me.*

***

"Alerac O'Neill has Keira at his compound. The wolf has his whole pack around her, and they're going to be guarding her constantly." Lorcan Teague stalked around the small room, circling the human. "It's now show time for you, Heath. Time to prove just how much you want that precious immortality." Heath Myers was sweating as he sat at the small table. "I can do this," the doctor said, his words a fast rush. "If I can talk to her, I can convince her that I'm on her side. That I'm trying to help her."

They were only an hour away from Alerac's home on the mountain. Lorcan didn't dare go any closer. He wasn't sure where Alerac would have his guards positioned. Some of those dogs could catch a scent from miles away.

"It's not going to be just a matter of walking to the gates and getting instant admission," Lorcan murmured.

Heath's shoulders straightened. "I-I don't smell like a vampire."

Don't you?

"I'm just human. All I need to do is get close to them. If Jane sees me, she won't let the werewolves hurt me."

The guy was an idiot. "You think that woman controls the werewolf alpha?" Laughable.

"I think—I think Jane will listen to me." Sweat leaked down Heath's temple. "Just give me this chance, okay? I can get to her."

Lorcan stilled. Then he leaned over the table. He made sure that Heath saw the threat in his eyes. "It's not about getting to her. It's about Keira coming to *me*." They needed to be very, very clear on this point. In two hundred years, no other blood princess had been born to his clan. They were too damn rare.

When he'd first learned that Keira had defiled herself with that wolf, his rage had nearly driven him mad.

But two hundred years had passed. The world had changed. There had been a few more werewolf and vampire matings over the years. He'd heard of those instances.

And been surprised by their results.

It seemed that when a vampire and werewolf bonded, when they shared blood, they also shared power.

Lorcan liked power. *I will be the strongest vampire to walk this earth.* He'd ruled his clan. Now it was time to rule all the vamps. It was *his* time.

He needed Keira back under his control because he wanted to study her. Heath wasn't the only doctor at his beck and call. Sure, magic was still his favorite pet, but Lorcan had also learned the value of science.

On its own, Keira's blood was useless to him. The power was only active when she bonded with the werewolf.

So I let the werewolf have you, for a time. He could have taken Keira from that little bar at any point. He hadn't. He'd waited. He'd *let* Alerac get to her because he needed for those two to exchange blood once more.

He was sure that the werewolf had given into his hunger for Keira by now.

So I have to get the blood now. The blood, and Keira.

Since making the discovery about the vampire and werewolf matings, Lorcan had drained his share of werewolves. He had received a slight strength increase from that wolf blood, but nothing like what the stories *said* the mated pairs enjoyed.

Lorcan didn't want a sliver of power. He wanted everything.

Keira was his key.

"You get to her," he told Heath and he smiled, letting his fangs flash. "Or you die." Simple fact. Either the werewolves would kill the doctor for stumbling onto their land—

Or I'll kill the fool when he fails.

Heath jumped to his feet. He hurried for the door. But then, he stopped. Glancing over his shoulder, the doctor said, "When I do this, when I bring her to you, promise that you'll turn me then."

Hell, no, he wasn't turning this prick. But he vaguely remembered making some sort of offer, so he just said, "Of course."

Heath's eyes became suspicious slits. Maybe he wasn't as dumb as he appeared.

"You'll live forever, never aging, never changing," Lorcan murmured, with a bored wave of his hand, "once Keira is brought back to me."

Heath nodded and reached for the door once more.

"Not so fast," Lorcan said. This was going to be the fun part. "If you go running to them with a sob story about me, you have to at least look as if you suffered a bit while in captivity."

The color bleached from Heath's skin.

"If you go to them all hale and hearty, then they'll never believe you were my prisoner."

The human's pulse was racing.

"So, let's make sure they believe," Lorcan said. "Let's make real sure."

He attacked.

***

"We have traitors in our midst." Alerac's voice boomed out into the night. He wanted to clear the air, fuckin' then. If any others had turned on him, Alerac wanted to face them.

The werewolves—all in human form—were gathered around him. At his announcement, there were uneasy murmurs from the group.

Jane stood just behind Alerac, with her brother close at her side.

Ryan. That man was going to keep being a fuckin' thorn in his side.

But Alerac owed him. Because it seemed that Ryan had saved Jane's life at that stream.

"What do you mean, traitors?" Finn demanded, his eyes narrowed and his brow furrowed.

"Liam attacked my mate tonight. He took her blood. He tried to take *her* from me." The rage was still there. The rage and the pain of betrayal. Liam had been at his side for so long. How had he missed this? *How?* "Three werewolves were with him. Saul. Benjamin, and Mitchell." He let his gaze sweep the group. "Those three are dead, killed by my claws, but Liam escaped."

Because Alerac had made a choice. Track Liam or follow Jane's scent. He'd followed Jane.

More murmurs and whispers swept through the group.

Did they doubt what he was telling them?

Yes.

Fuck, yes, they did.

Finn stepped forward. "We don't like having vampires in our midst!"

There were nods. Growls of agreement. They growled, even when in the form of men and women.

Suspicious stares were cast toward Jane and Ryan.

"Maybe Ben and Saul were the ones attacked," Finn added. "Maybe your vamp was the one to—"

Alerac had him by the throat before he could say anything more. "You question my word? The word of your alpha?"

Finn couldn't speak to respond, mostly because Alerac was crushing the guy's windpipe.

But Finn did manage to shake his head — *no.*

"No one threatens Jane and lives." Simple. His word — his pack law. He released Finn. The guy sucked in a deep breath.

Suspicion churned within Alerac. He'd been blind to Liam's betrayal. Was he still being blind now? "If there are others helping Liam, siding with him, I will learn the truth."

There weren't any murmurs then. Just considering glances. No, those were suspicious glances. The wolves seemed to weigh each other.

"I brought you here," Alerac said, voice strong and cold. "I created this pack. If any of you think to turn on me — then challenge me, *now.* Come at me. See if you have what it takes to be alpha." Because he was sure ready to kick the shit out of someone.

Only none of the wolves approached him.

Their heads lowered in submission.

He'd found these wolves over the years. They'd been alone, lost. He'd brought them together.

No, not just me. Liam was at my side. Would the wolves feel they owed their allegiance to him?

Or to Liam?

His gaze swept the group once more. Stopped on a pair of angry brown eyes.

Zoe. She and Finn were the two newest members of the pack. Finn had seemed to fit in with the others instantly, but Zoe had remained aloof.

Zoe wasn't like the others. She was a werewolf who couldn't shift. The beast within her had never been able to push its way out, not completely.

Zoe's dark hair was still wet from the storm. The rain had stopped just minutes ago. "You called her your mate!" A faint southern accent whispered beneath Zoe's words. "Is that what she is?"

To Alerac, Jane had been his mate for centuries. But he glanced back at Jane.

She was staring at him in confusion.

"Vampires make us nervous," another werewolf called out. "We follow your orders, but, alpha, we need to know just who you are bringing into our pack."

He should have known that it would come to this. Fear could live in the heart of any man. Or beast.

"Is she your mate?" Zoe pressed. "Because I don't remember a claiming."

"Maybe that's why Liam went after her." The words came from another werewolf. Denton.

"Maybe he wanted a claim. I can smell him on her."

Claws burst from Alerac's hands. In an instant, he'd slashed that jerk. Denton had always been a mouthy SOB. "The only *scent* on her is mine. Just because Liam attacked her, it doesn't give him a claim."

"Alerac…" Jane's voice was soft, worried.

But it was Zoe's hand that reached out to Alerac. She touched his shoulder. That light touch stopped him from killing Denton. "Maybe you should make a claim them," she told him quietly. Her eyes were worried. "A claim would reassure…" Zoe swallowed, and said, "*all* of us." Her eyes sent him the message that he needed to heed her words. "A public claiming is the way of the pack."

It was.

But he couldn't claim an unwilling bride.

"Oh, the hell, *no,*" Ryan snarled, leaping toward them. "This dog isn't mating with *my* — "

Four werewolves closed in on him.

Alerac lifted his hand. "Stop."

They stopped.

Dammit. He should have seen this problem before. Zoe was trying to help him. He got that. To reassure his pack — the pack that remained in the middle of this freakin' mutiny — he needed to claim his vampire. Then the others wouldn't be so worried that she was going to turn on them.

Or…um, feed on them.

She only drinks from me.

"Jane." He hadn't meant to shout her name but this wasn't exactly the time for endearments and soft promises.

He wasn't the type for those promises anyway.

Jane didn't step toward him. She just stared back at him. Hell, if she rejected him in front of his pack, what would he do then?

He turned his back on the wolves. Then hesitated. "Don't kill the male vampire. Not yet."

"Don't worry." Zoe pushed through the crowd that had surrounded Ryan. "I'll keep him alive." She positioned herself in front of a frowning Ryan.

"I don't need *your* protection," Ryan muttered.

"Right, Drac. Whatever you say."

Satisfied that Ryan would keep living — for the moment — Alerac eliminated the distance between him and Jane.

"What's going on?" Jane asked him. Her neck had healed, but Zoe was right. Liam's scent was on her.

Bastard. You will suffer for this.

Liam had gone right after the one thing that Alerac valued most. *Why?*

"I called you my mate in front of the pack." He wasn't even sure that had been an accident.

Maybe he'd realized, deep down, exactly what he was doing. "The wolves are nervous about having a vampire here."

"Two vampires," she said, voice soft.

He nodded. "And with three of their own dead, they need reassurance."

Her lashes lowered, concealing her gaze.

"If you accept my claim, then you're part of the pack. You're part of *me*."

"And if I don't?"

He'd look like a fool. He'd also have to fight all of the werewolves who wanted to go for her throat and for Ryan's. "Then I'll make sure you get a safe escort to wherever you want to go." There was no need for her to know the rest.

Her lashes lifted. "What is a werewolf claiming? Does it mean we're — we're dating?"

No. "It's like marriage." Only there was no divorce for them. No out clause. The claiming was forever. Beyond life and death.

"You're asking me to marry you?" He could see himself reflected in her eyes. A scary sight. Why the hell would she want to be saddled with him?

She was already afraid of him, and she didn't even know half of the things that he'd done in his life.

"I'm asking you to trust me." His voice was low, but he knew the others would still be able to overhear him. "I've protected you so far. I want to keep you safe."

But then she made the breath leave his lungs. Made his heart damn near burst from his chest.

She shook her head. "I want more than safety."

Hell. "What do you want?" He would try to give it to her. He would try—

"I want my life back."

Ice encased his skin.

The werewolves began to whisper behind him. He prepared for battle. The first wolf that attacked her would lose a limb.

He straightened his shoulders. He'd been the one to take her life away. He'd be the one to make sure she got it back. That she got everything back. "Just stay behind me," he told her. "It's about to get bloody."

He turned away.

She touched him. Wrapped her fingers around his arm, just as Zoe had done. Only when Zoe touched him, his blood hadn't heated. His body hadn't tensed. Need hadn't pounded through him as his beast clamored for escape.

For her.

"You're about to fight them all?"

Silence from the wolves. They had to be tensing for battle, too.

"But…" Now Jane sounded confused. "They're your family. They didn't all attack me. It was just the ones in the woods."

Maybe. But if he didn't claim her, they'd grow more suspicious of her. Vampires and werewolves had a very long blood feud going.

One that wasn't ending overnight. His claim would protect her.

Without it, he'd make sure that his claws and teeth did the job.

Her hold tightened on him. "Don't do this."

She'd taken his choice away.

Alerac pulled from her. Kept his spine straight and his chin up as he met the stares of his pack. His claim had just been publicly refused. That should have been humiliating.

It wasn't.

He just…his chest hurt.

Alerac lifted his claws. "Who's going to be first?" He was alpha for a reason. He'd prove that fact again this night. Before the sun rose, their blood would be on the ground. Jane would be safe.

He did a "come here" motion with his claws. "Let's get started."

"No!" Jane's yell.

And then Jane was there. In front of him. Grabbing his wrists. Pushing her body against his. "You're not doing this for me!"

Yes, he was. He wasn't going to let her be threatened.

Jane shook her head. "No, not for me." Her pulse raced. He could smell the fear that drifted from her.

He didn't like the scent of fear on Jane.

He preferred the sweet scent of her desire.

"I accept your claim."

He liked it when—

What?

"Did you hear me?" Her eyes searched his. "There's no need to fight. No need to turn on your own. I accept your claim."

"Fuck," Ryan muttered.

Her fingers were stroking the inside of his wrists. She was trying to soothe him. He wasn't in the mood to be soothed.

She'd just accepted his claim. That changed *everything.*

"What happens now?" Her voice was a breathless whisper.

"Now..." Alerac turned her in his arms, positioning her so that all would see just what was coming. "I take you. I make you *mine.*"

CHAPTER EIGHT

She was a creature straight from some kid's nightmare. A blood-drinker. An immortal power.

And her knees were shaking.

Alerac's hard body pressed behind her. She could feel the strong muscles of his chest. The ripple of his cut abs. He hadn't bothered with a shirt, so it was all too easy to feel the strength of his bare muscles against her.

He'd jerked on a pair of jeans. And his cock was, ah, definitely getting bigger and harder behind her.

Everyone was staring at her.

"Uh, Alerac…" She wasn't sure just how the werewolves did things, but putting on a show for the pack wasn't her idea of a good time.

"Do you accept my claim?" His voice seemed to thunder behind her.

Jane nodded.

Then she jumped when she felt his breath whisper against her ear. "You have to say the words, *a rúnsearc*."

Oh. Okay. "I accept your claim."

The werewolves started shouting then. She wasn't sure if those were celebrating shouts or we-want-to-kill-her shouts.

It was too hard to tell the difference.

That whisper of his breath slid away from her ear as his mouth moved down to her neck.

Jane couldn't help it. She tensed even more. The memory of Liam holding her down and tearing into her throat was far too fresh in her mind.

"Trust me."

She wanted to trust Alerac.

"It will only hurt for an instant."

"Wait—" Jane began.

But it was too late. His teeth sank into her. Not her throat, but right at the curve of her shoulder. It did hurt, but, like he'd said, the pain only lasted an instant. A white- hot pulse that charged through her body.

After that pain, *pleasure.* She gasped because she'd only been prepared for pain. Not for this.

More pulses of pleasure shot through her, starting right there, where his mouth was on her skin, and they surged down…straight down to her sex.

He was licking her. Kissing her skin.

And she was about to climax just from his mouth on her.

Horrified— *they're watching* — Jane spun in his arms.

Those arms closed tightly around her.

"It's done." His voice carried easily over the shouts. "She's mine."

That hadn't been so bad. She looked up at him. "And you're...*mine*."

"Keira!"

Her head jerked at Ryan's bellow. The werewolves were holding him back. Had the guy tried to lunge forward and stop the claiming?

Yes.

Zoe still stood in front of him. She was frowning up at Ryan. "Dumb, Drac, dumb."

"Don't do this!" Ryan yelled at Jane. "Don't trade your life again. Don't do it for me!"

She hadn't. Jane shook her head. "I did this for me."

Then she was being lifted up in Alerac's arms. He carried her into the main house. Before he crossed that threshold, he glanced back. "Zoe, keep the male vampire alive."

Zoe nodded.

Alerac glanced over at the rest of his pack. "Liam is banished. If you see him, take the bastard down. He will not hurt this pack again. Search the woods. Protect the borders. Do *not* turn your back on him."

Their faces were grim. Jane realized that they were all going to be hunting Liam now. He'd been a brother to them one moment, then a traitor the next.

Why? Alerac had trusted him. She was pretty sure Alerac had loved him.

As had the others.

Now there would be no room for love.

Only death.

Alerac turned from the assembled wolves. He carried her inside, and he shut the rest of the world.

***

"I guess that makes you think she's less," the small female said as she glared up at Ryan, "because your sister just tied herself to a vampire."

Ryan barred his fangs at her. Her scent…He shook his head, feeling a little drunk. Maybe that was just fury making him feel that way. Four werewolves were holding him in place—two on each side of him. If it hadn't been for their cutting grip, he would have rushed up and stopped Alerac long before the alpha claimed Keira.

"It was her choice," the woman continued. Her skin was the most delectable shade of dark cream that he'd ever seen. "Let it be, and you'll both be under pack protection."

Right. Like he gave a damn about that. "The same pack that attacked her just an hour ago?" He was tired of those SOBs holding him. His fangs were ready to rip and tear.

"Don't."

He frowned at her.

She shook her head. Then she pointed to the werewolves. "Let him go. I'll watch the vamp."

They let him go. Just like that.

The other werewolves were all backing away. The show was over, so they were gone? Forget that.

He stalked toward the main house's entrance.

"You don't want to interrupt him right now." She sighed and said, "Whether you're her brother or not, Alerac might just take your head if you interrupt the bonding ceremony."

Ryan halted. "I can take Alerac."

"Why? Because you're an ancient vampire?" She *rolled* her dark eyes. "Big deal. Alerac has killed plenty of those."

Yes, he had.

"You know he's not just a werewolf. Not anymore. Not thanks to her."

His sister had changed Alerac. That change made the alpha even more dangerous.

He turned his head. Found his gaze sliding right back to the woman. She was small and delicate, when werewolves were normally built along much harder, tougher lines. Her dark eyes were wide, almond shaped, and her full lips were set determinedly.

"Who are you?" Ryan demanded as he studied her. She looked young, barely twenty-five, but werewolves and their ages could be deceptive.

Not as deceptive as a vampire's age of course but…

"Zoe."

He lifted a brow.

"He won't hurt her. You know he can't." She glanced toward the sky. "The sun's rising soon. You need to get to shelter."

Shelter wasn't what he needed. "Keira is being hunted."

Zoe gave a little shrug as she headed away from him. "I think she calls herself Jane now."

He stared after her.

"Sunlight makes you weak, right? I wouldn't think you'd want the others to see you that way." She looked over her shoulder. "No one is letting you leave, by the way. So you can come willingly with me, or one of those guys—" She pointed toward the wolves who lingered near the edge of the woods. "Those guys will just lock you up until Alerac is ready to deal with you."

Deal with—

"He said we couldn't kill you, not that we couldn't hurt you." She wasn't looking at him any longer. "After the pain vampires have inflicted on this pack, there are plenty of werewolves looking for some payback."

"I'm not afraid of some mangy wolves."

The words were barely out of his mouth before he found claws at his throat. Her claws. "Maybe you should be," Zoe snapped.

He smiled at her—and knocked those claws away. In the next breath, she was trapped in his arms, and his teeth were inches from her throat. Her scent—so heady, so tempting—dared him to take a bite.

But when he looked up, he saw the wolves circling in on him.

Ryan let her go. Except...he didn't want to.

He wanted to bite.

He locked his teeth. "I'll stay with you for today. You keep your claws off me, and I'll keep my teeth out of you."

Maybe. He'd try.

She was just...tempting.

"Do we have a deal?" Ryan pushed.

She smiled at him. The woman actually flashed dimples as she said, "I don't make deals with vampires."

He didn't usually want to fuck werewolves.

"But I think we can avoid killing each other until nightfall."

Sounded like a plan.

He followed her away from the main house, enjoying the sway of her ass. A very nice ass, one that was encased in tight jeans.

"Are you this fierce when you shift into a beast?" Ryan asked her, curious. Because if she was, the woman would be one dangerous killing machine.

She stopped at the door of a two-story cabin, one with a row of flowers growing on its side. Pain flickered over her face. "No, I'm not."

"I don't know if I believe that."

Her gaze slashed up to meet his. "Believe it. What you see is what you get." Zoe swallowed. "I don't shift. I can't."

A werewolf who couldn't shift? He stared after her, and he felt shame. Shame that he'd attacked her. Shame that he'd made her hurt and—

"Get your ass in here, Drac, before you burn."

He got his ass in that cabin.

*****

Heath stared at the pool of blood on the floor. His blood. Just inches from his face.

He should move. Get up. Run.

But he just felt so weak.

A door opened. Closed. Footsteps came into the room. Soft, rustling.

"Hello, witch." That was Lorcan's rough voice.

The footsteps stopped. Heath managed to turn his head, just a few inches, and he saw the woman.

No, not just a normal woman, a witch.

She was beautiful, with golden hair and deep eyes. But those eyes looked wrong—*broken.*

His gaze slid to her neck, and to the deep marks there. Would he soon bear similar scars?

Lorcan destroys everything that he touches.

The witch stared down at Heath. Pity softened her face. "I thought you were going to let him live."

"I am." Lorcan just sounded bored. He usually did. "Don't worry, my dear, I didn't drain him dry. He'll be able to pull himself off the floor soon enough."

The legs of a chair screeched as they were shoved across the wooden floor. Then Lorcan appeared. He wrapped his hands around the witch. Pulled her close.

The vampire acted as if he didn't even feel the flinch that shook her. "Do you have the cure?" he asked as he bent to lick the woman's neck.

The pain had lessened in Heath's neck. What cure?

"I do," she said. Her eyes didn't actually look broken so much as dead.

"Once she discovers that she has a brother, Keira—I mean, Jane—will pay dearly for that cure."

Jane had a brother?

I can use that. I can use this cure. Heath kept his body still on the floor, not wanting to draw Lorcan's attention.

"Pity for her," Lorcan muttered, "that she didn't get the cure sooner. Now it's time for Ryan to die. Time for him to burn." He laughed then. "And he will burn, from the inside, out. He'll die screaming. He won't even last another full day."

Lorcan freed the witch. He stalked toward Heath and kicked him in the ribs. "And, human, it's time for you to finish our deal. Go get Jane. Bring her to me."

Heath crawled for the door. And, with every painful inch, he planned.

***

She'd chosen him. *Him.*

Alerac kicked the bedroom door shut behind him. His hands were shaking. The control he'd kept so carefully was being torn to shreds.

Jane waited in the middle of the bedroom. Her arms were by her sides and her feet shifted nervously. "Ah, what happens now?"

Now he took her.

But first…Alerac cleared his throat, and tried to speak with the voice of the man. Hard, when the beast was clawing his way to freedom. "You have to bite me."

Her sensual lips parted. "I-I already have."

He shook his head. "That was different. That was about survival. This time, it's for bonding." He crossed to her. His fingers lifted, and his thumb pressed against her lips.

She stared at him, and the darkness spread in her eyes.

"You drink from me so that we can be linked."

Her breath blew lightly over his thumb. "I'll get more of your memories."

"Yes." That didn't matter to him. She'd chosen to be his mate, so there was no going back now. He wanted her to know all of him. Good. Bad. Everything gray that fell between.

No matter what she saw in his memories, he would find a way to prove to Jane that he could be better. That their life together could be a happy one.

Her fangs were growing. Maybe he shouldn't have found vampire fangs sexy. He did, but only on her.

"Go ahead." He invited her as he forced his hand to drop. "Bite me."

Her fingers rose and pressed against his chest. The palm of her right hand was just over his tattoo, and the mark seemed to burn at her touch.

"What is this?" Jane asked. Her gaze had fallen on the edges of that tattoo. "How do you even have it? I would think that when you shift, it would vanish."

"It's a special tattoo." And it had taken two days to get it. Two days of gut-wrenching pain. Because she was right—a normal tattoo would have vanished with his shift. "A witch made a magic ink for me. One that would last forever."

He didn't tell her what the Celtic knot meant, not then. Alerac didn't reveal that the tattoo itself was a symbol of forever, that the corners symbolized his search. North. South. East. West. He'd vowed to search every corner of the earth.

For her.

She'd already accepted his claim. In that moment, he just wanted to focus on the present. On making sure the bond that they created was strong.

Her eyes met his. "I don't want to hurt you."

"You won't."

"When Liam bit me…" Her body trembled. "It hurt. I don't want to do that to you."

"When you bite me, it's not about pain." His fingers slid down her body. Gripped her slender waist. "Only pleasure."

"Promise?"

"I fuckin' vow it."

Jane gave a small nod. Then she rose onto her toes. Her mouth was on his throat. *Yes.* He felt the lick of her tongue. The caress of her lips.

The bite of her teeth.

His control shattered as the pleasure pumped through him.

He pulled her tighter against him. Held her closer. His cock was fully erect, desperate to thrust inside of her. *He* was desperate.

Her mouth on him…the pleasure was almost as strong as the release he found when he was thrusting into her body.

He shoved down her jeans. She kicked them away, along with her shoes.

He tore her underwear. Tossed it.

Her mouth was still on him.

He wanted *in* her.

He lifted her lips. Jane's legs wrapped around him. Her tongue pressed over his skin. She was lifting her teeth—

"Don't stop," he ordered. Or maybe he begged.

He took two steps. The bed was too far. He pushed her back against the nearest wall. Held her in his arms. Drove as deep into her as he could go.

He filled her. Every single inch of her hot core. She was tight and wet, and he had no control. None.

He was holding her too tightly. Driving in to her too deeply. But he couldn't stop.

Again and again, he thrust into her. Deeper. Harder. More.

She came, bucking against him, and her mouth pulled from his as she cried out his name.

Her sex clenched around him, spasming with her release. Those milking contractions propelled him to his own climax. He thrust hard into her. And erupted.

The pleasure blazed through him, consuming him from the inside out.

Her breath heaved out. So did his. Alerac's heartbeat raced in his chest.

He looked down at her. Jane's eyes were wide, her face flushed with pleasure.

"We're not done." Not even close. But at least he'd taken the edge off. Now he could make it to the bed, and he did. He carried her toward the four-poster. Made sure not to let his claws hurt her skin.

He eased her down on the covers. She started to lie down on her back.

"No."

He turned her onto her stomach. Put her hands down. Lifted her onto her knees. She glanced back at him. "Alerac?"

"I need you this way." Gravel-rough.

Her gaze fell to this cock. "You didn't—"

"I did." And he was about to, again. He pushed into her, and she was slick and swollen from her release. Thrusting into her right then was better than the best dream he'd ever had.

Her fingers clenched the bed covers. A moan spilled from her throat.

He covered her with his body. Alerac put his mouth on her shoulder. He'd marked her there, in front of the pack. Now he'd mark her while they were alone.

In and out. He thrust slowly, holding back the pleasure. In. Out.

It was his turn to lick her skin. To taste her. Not just as a werewolf, but as the being he'd become, because of her.

Part wolf.

Part vampire.

His teeth sank into her.

Her hips shoved back against him. "Alerac!" A demand this time.

He met that demand. His thrusts shook her. Shook the bed. Could have shaken the whole damn house for all he cared.

Her blood was on his tongue. His cock in her snug sex. He surrounded her.

She fuckin' enslaved him.

She came, shuddering, and she ripped the covers with her grip.

He kept thrusting. Driving into her as deeply as he could go. He'd been kept apart from her for far too long. He'd had too many empty nights, too many dreams of her. He'd woken, alone, lost, bellowing her name.

She was with him now. Linked, bound, forever.

There was no escape.

His release was even stronger this time. His heart nearly burst from him as held her tighter.

No escape.

Because, if he lost her again, Alerac knew he'd go mad.

***

"I'll take his punishment."

The words were soft, almost broken.

They were her words.

Jane could see herself, a small figure surrounded by angry vampires. She was staring straight ahead and offering to take someone's—

"No! You can't!"

Those words…that was Alerac's voice.

She looked down and saw a knife hanging from her chest. No, not her chest—*Alerac's.*

This was his memory. She was seeing everything from his point of view again.

The knife was yanked from him. The silver burned, and smoke drifted up from the wound. Then the blade was pushed against Alerac's throat.

A vampire stood there, eyes shining as he glared down at Alerac. His dark hair was swept back from his high forehead. His lips twisted in disgust. "The punishment is death," the dark vampire said. "He came here, he *used* you, in order to get into our midst. To attack us from within."

Wait—that vampire had to be the one Alerac had warned her about—Lorcan. That guy was obviously the boss in this little nightmare scene.

She'd expected him to look like a monster. He didn't. He was handsome, seemingly in the bloom of his youth. It was only when he looked deeply into Alerac's eyes that she could see the flare of evil.

"I-I've started turning."

"When," Lorcan demanded to know.

"Y-yesterday."

The knife was lifted from Alerac's throat. His hands clenched as he pulled at the silver manacles that bound him.

"He used you!" Lorcan snapped. Alerac's blood dripped from the knife. "And yet you would give your life for him? *Why?*"

She didn't respond right away.

"*Why?*" Lorcan's shout filled the chamber.

"Because I love him."

Lorcan smiled, but it was a cold and cruel sight. "You can't die for him, Keira. You have too much value to us." A pause. "But you can take his punishment. After all, you were the one to bring him in to our clan. A dog, walking among gods."

"You're no god," Alerac snarled.

Lorcan's eyes narrowed. "One hundred years. That's the penalty for treason in our clan. Imprisonment. Starvation. For one hundred years."

One hundred years. How could even a vampire survive that long without some kind of food? Because he'd said starvation—

"I will take the punishment, but you have to promise me that Alerac lives. No matter what else happens, he *lives.*"

"Why?" Lorcan's lips were twisted into a sly smile. "By the time you are free, he'll be long dead."

"Swear it, Lorcan. Vow it to me on the blood."

Lorcan's gaze returned to Alerac. "I vow it," he agreed.

The vampires hauled her away. Shackles were put around her wrists as Alerac watched, and something...broke in him. He lunged to his feet, roaring, as his beast pushed for freedom. He yanked the manacles from the wall.

The images vanished into a swirl of darkness.

For once, Jane preferred the darkness. Fear was acid in her gut, churning, destroying.

But the darkness didn't last.

New images slipped before her. The dark haired vampire—Lorcan. She knew him now.

Knew him through Alerac's memories. He was the bastard who had imprisoned her.

Then he was before her. No, not before her, but before Alerac. Another vision, another one starring Lorcan. He was smiling his twisted, evil grin.

"I said you would get to live." Lorcan bent and picked up the silver knife. "But I never vowed that you would not suffer."

Another vampire yanked back Alerac's head.

"I think I'll start with your eyes," Lorcan said. "After all, what good is a wolf who cannot see?"

The blade came toward him. The silver burned and cut and the pain rolled through him.

In her mind, Jane was screaming. She was crying. She was so desperate to escape that silver knife.

She didn't see Lorcan any longer. She saw red—blood.

Then she saw nothing.

***

"*No!*" Jane reached for her eyes, sobbing. She'd been sentenced to a lifetime of darkness. She hadn't meant—

"Jane?"

Her breath froze.

His fingers wrapped around her wrists. "What's wrong?"

She didn't lower her hands. "I saw more of your memories." She was sure starting to think that she was far better off without the knowledge of the past.

The past freaking terrified her.

Jane forced herself to take a deep breath. Then she lowered her hands. "Lorcan…"

"You saw him in the visions?"

Saw him, and would never be able to forget that SOB. He'd enjoyed hurting her—and Alerac. Jane nodded. "I saw what he did…to you." She looked into his eyes, those glowing eyes that didn't belong to a man.

But to the beast.

"He took your eyes."

Alerac's chest was bare. The sheet tangled around his waist. He leaned over her, caging her against the covers.

Her hand lifted to his cheek. "*He took your eyes.*"

He caught her hand. "Don't worry, I plan to take a hell of a lot more from him."

Was that supposed to make her feel better? It didn't. "Is that why your eyes glow?"

"I lost the eyes of the man." No emotion was in his voice. "When a werewolves shifts, the beasts heal our injuries. When I finally healed, the beast gave me even better eyes than I'd had before. Stronger. Sharper."

Finally healed. "How long did it take you to heal?"

"Long enough."

That wasn't an answer.

"It doesn't matter." Now there was emotion sliding through his mask as he eased away from her.

She thought it did matter. "One hundred years." That had been the punishment determined by Lorcan. "You searched for me, all that time?"

"No."

She blinked.

"It was *two* hundred years. After you took the knife and stabbed Lorcan," a wry smile curved his lips as he seemed to recall the memory, "he got pissed and upped your sentence."

She'd stabbed the guy.

Good.

The two hundred years part? Not so good. Yet somehow that didn't bother her as much as the fact that… "He cut out your eyes. I-I thought you were supposed to be protected." The vampiress in her vision — Keira, *me* — she'd wanted to protect Alerac. Not get him tortured.

Alerac rose from the bed. He walked toward the closet.

Nice ass.

He hauled on a pair of jeans and destroyed her nice view. "You were more important than my damn eyes." He turned back to face her. "My pack was coming. We had planned a dawn attack on the vampires. You should have still been there at the keep. They would have gotten you out. Gotten me free. I would have killed Lorcan—"

"Why didn't you kill him?" She pulled the covers over her breasts.

His hand rose and pressed against the tattoo that covered his heart. "Because he was the only one who knew where you were. He sent men to hide you, to lock you up, and then his witch killed them."

She didn't remember meeting any witches, but, even so, the very idea of them was making her plenty nervous.

"I had to let Lorcan live as long as you were trapped. He was the only one that would be able to free you. That fuckin' bastard. I dreamed of killin' him, again and again." His accent thickened a bit as his hand dropped. "Now I can. You're safe, and he's about to be minus a head."

She hurried from the bed. "All of the other vampires—did you kill them for vengeance?"

Those images were still in her head, too. Alerac, soaked in blood. Alerac, feeding on them.

He stared back at her. "They were allied with Lorcan. I thought they might know where you were." His lips twisted. "You aren't the only one who can drink memories, you know."

Her lips parted but she wasn't sure what to say then.

"You changed me." His voice was low. "I planned to use you. Fuck, you think I like admitting it? Seduce the vampiress, then use her to get inside the castle."

Wasn't that exactly what he'd done?

"Something changed." He wasn't touching her. She found that she couldn't touch him.

I love you.

She'd told him that. When they were surrounded by vampires. When she'd traded her life for his.

But he hadn't given her the same words.

"I planned to destroy all of the vampires in that clan, but not you. *Not you.* I was going to take you with me."

"You'd had my blood." And he'd realized that it made him stronger?

He gave a grim nod. "But more than that, I'd had *you.*"

"Alerac—"

Then she heard the shouts from outside. Angry. Desperate. In the next instant, she and Alerac were both running to the window.

The sun was still out, and it should have weakened her when she pressed open that glass.

It didn't. Just as it hadn't weakened her when she'd been on that motorcycle with him.

Because of his blood? Alerac had told her the truth. It sure seemed as if she'd built up some kind of immunity to the sunlight, thanks to him.

She saw Zoe and Finn. They were rushing toward the main cabin, with — with *Heath* between them?

"What the hell is he doing here?" Alerac demanded.

"Jane!" Heath shouted, looking up at that same moment. Blood dripped down his face and neck. "Help me!"

She started to race down to him.

"No." Alerac wrapped his hand around her wrist. "He's working for Lorcan."

Heath looked as if he were dying.

Alerac's gaze found hers. "We'll see him together. I want to discover just what game the doc thinks he's playing."

"What if it's not a game? What if he just needs help?"

"He sold you out before." His eyes narrowed. "As far as I'm concerned, that's a killing crime."

She glanced back down at Heath's slumped figure. To her, it appeared as if someone had already tried to kill him.

And, if Heath didn't get help soon, he might not survive much longer at all.

CHAPTER NINE

Zoe and Finn dropped Heath on the floor. The doc hit the wood and moaned. A pitiful sound.

An annoying sound.

Jane attempted to hurry toward the guy.

Smothering a sigh, Alerac just blocked her path.

"Would you stop that?" Jane snapped at him.

No, he wouldn't, because he didn't trust the guy. "You searched him for weapons?" Alerac demanded of Zoe and Finn.

Zoe glanced up at him. "No guns. No knives. No stakes." Her nose wrinkled. "Just a bloody and beat-up human."

"Where'd you find him?"

"He was dumped on the south side of our land," Finn answered quickly. "Found him when I was patrolling to make sure Liam hadn't come back."

Dumped—or delivered?

"Pl-please…" Heath muttered. "Help…"

Jane shoved Alerac out of her way and knelt next to the doctor. She turned him over, and when she got a good look at his face, Jane gasped.

His nose had been broken. His left eye was swollen shut. Blood dripped from his mouth— *aw, did the doc lose some teeth?* — and gaping wounds covered his throat.

"He's…insane…" Heath whispered. "You…you have to help me…"

Zoe and Finn were still standing close by.

"You need to be taken to a hospital," Jane said. She looked over at Zoe. "We're going to need a car to transport him."

Heath grabbed her hand.

Alerac tensed. *You're about to lose that hand.*

"N-no, hospital. I'd—I'd have to explain…the bites…"

"You're hurt. You need help," Jane told him. "You could die!"

"N-need blood…"

The hell, *no.*

Alerac marched forward. He grabbed Heath and hauled the guy to his feet. "Tell me that you're not this much of a dumbass."

The man blinked at him.

"You don't seriously think," Alerac continued, letting his disgust show, "that you can drag your carcass in here, after what you've done, and get *blood* from Jane?"

"D-dying…" Heath whispered pitifully.

"Bull." The wounds actually seemed to already be…healing.

Healing as Alerac stared at them.

Suspicion churned in his gut. "You bastard."

Heath tried to pull free.

Alerac wasn't letting him go. "You were her doctor, her *friend,* for these last six months. She trusted you—and you…you took her blood, didn't you?"

Heath was fighting to get free now.

Alerac turned his bright stare on Jane. "He took your blood." Certainty. Rage.

She rose to her feet. After a moment, Jane gave a faint nod. "Samples. He said that he needed them for tests."

Alerac shook his head. "No, he needed the blood for its power." He lifted Heath up into the air, and the smaller man dangled above the floor. "You think I don't know your type? Greedy, desperate, willing to trade anyone and everyone for the promise of immortality?"

Heath stopped looking quite so beaten. His lips twisted in a hard snarl. "Isn't that what you did when *you* took her blood? Werewolves aren't supposed to live as long as you have. You found out that vamp blood can extend your life. You found—"

Alerac's claws were out. "This is the part where you die."

"No!" Jane jumped forward. "Dammit, *no!*

Heath started to smile.

But then Jane continued, "We can't kill him yet. We have to find out what he knows about Lorcan first."

That wiped Heath's smile away.

Alerac nodded. Then he said, "Finn, get some rope. I want to make sure this SOB is tied up tight."

Heath was fighting now. Too late.

Jane stared at him, anger coursing through her veins. "You really were just going to sell me out that night, weren't you? Just hand me right over to Lorcan—"

"Not to Lorcan, not then." He huffed out a hard breath. "To the other werewolf."

Rage nearly choked Alerac then. "*Liam.*"

A frantic nod from Heath. "H-he was the one I called. He arranged for the guys in those SUVs to meet us." His words tumbled over each other. "Man, I swear, I didn't even know Lorcan then."

Then. Alerac dropped the bastard to the floor. "So when did you make Lorcan's fine acquaintance?"

Heath didn't rise from the floor. He curled in on himself. "A-after. The men who were left...they were trying to figure out how to get Jane—"

Alerac growled.

Heath flinched. "But Lorcan found us first. It was like hell came at them. Lorcan broke into the house, and he killed them all in seconds. Every last one. He took their heads." A thick swallow. "Their organs."

Same old twisted Lorcan.

"But he let you live?" The question came from a doubting Zoe. "Your story is crap."

Heath's head lifted. His eyes slid toward Jane. "He smelled your blood on me. He let me live because of that. I told him that we were friends. Th-that I could help him to find you."

"No," Alerac wanted to rip him apart, "what you told him was that you'd betray Jane, that you'd sell her out." And he already had a pretty good idea of the price that Heath would have demanded. "Let me guess. You're gonna trade Jane for immortality?" Probably a fat wad of cash, too.

Heath shook his head. "No! You don't understand!" His eyes locked on Jane. "He doesn't want to kill you! You're part of his clan. He just wants you back."

***

They'd taken the human inside.

Lorcan smiled. Either Jane would trust the doctor—or Heath would die.

When he'd first found Heath, the human had been so desperate. Crying. Begging.

Once, Lorcan had enjoyed it when his prey begged. Now it just bored him.

But he'd spared Heath because Lorcan had known that he could use the human as a distraction, at the right time.

The time is right now.

He lifted his hand to his throat. It still ached, but the pain was more of a memory. Lorcan had long ago grown used to pain—both giving it and taking it. He'd made sure that the doctor enjoyed plenty of pain before Heath had been allowed to venture to Jane's side.

He knew what was happening inside that wolf pack. The betrayal. The battle.

Liam had turned on Alerac. He'd thought the two wolves were as close as brothers. But even a brother would kill you if there was enough power involved.

Lorcan had killed both of his brothers centuries ago. A witch had come to Lorcan long before he'd ever tasted his first sip of blood. She'd told him that his brothers were destined to destroy him.

He'd destroyed them first. As their blood had soaked the ground beneath his feet, he'd learned just how valuable a witch could be.

A witch's power could change the world.

And the right vampire—he could *rule* the paranormal world.

Normally, he wouldn't give a damn about werewolf politics, but Liam had crossed the line. He'd *hurt* Jane.

Twice, Liam had sent vampires after her.

My own damn kind. The knowledge still burned.

Those vampires could have killed Jane. They hadn't realized just what an immense mistake they were making.

No one could kill Jane. She belonged to him. Not just as a clansman, but so much more.

He was the only one left who remembered the bond that had been forged so long ago. Perhaps it was time for him to enlighten the others.

For them to truly see that there was no hope for Jane and Alerac. The lovers weren't going to get some romantic, happy ending.

It was too late for that.

Jane was already linked to another, through blood and pain, until death.

***

"He doesn't want to kill you! You're part of his clan. He just wants you back."

Right. Jane didn't buy that line for an instant. Not with the images of Lorcan still swirling in her mind.

Finn came back into the room, holding thick rope in his hands. Alerac dumped Heath into the nearest chair, and they tied him up tight. Tight enough to cut off the circulation.

Then Alerac backed up. He cocked a brow and glanced at Jane. "Want to go first?"

Yeah, she had plenty of questions for her *friend.* "How did you know to find me in that swamp?" When she'd been walking alone, covered in dirt and grime. Her mind broken. Her body convulsing from hunger. "It wasn't some vacation trip. Some coincidence."

Heath's gaze glanced around, sweeping the room.

"Don't expect Liam to come to your aid," Alerac snapped at him. "The pack knows he's a traitor. He's been hunted now."

Heath's Adam's apple bobbed.

"*Tell me!*" Jane demanded.

"L-Liam told me where to find you. Said he'd drunk the memory from some vamp years ago. The enchantment that held you prisoner was supposed to fall away this year, and he figured that if you were strong enough, you'd crawl your way to freedom."

"Where was she?" Alerac's voice was low.

In his binds, Heath shrugged. Some blood still dripped from his wounds. "All I know is she dug her way out of a grave in that swamp."

A grave. "I was buried alive? All that time?"

Another shrug.

"How could even a vampire survive that?" Zoe asked as sympathy flashed across her face. "Wouldn't you need food? Air? I mean, you breathe, right?"

"It was the spell," Alerac said, voice wooden. "It locked in the air in her lungs, froze her body, and made it her prison. She could feel the bloodlust and hunger, but she couldn't move." His face was tight with fury. "Magic can do anything, if it's strong enough." Alerac yanked his hand through his hair. "*Liam knew.*"

Jane tried to focus on breathing. She'd been shoved in the ground somewhere out in that swamp, buried alive for all of those years? A prisoner, in her own body. *I don't want those memories back.* Maybe that made her a coward, but she didn't care. Screw the past. She was ready for the future.

"It was gift, you know?" Heath was staring at her now. "Once I went with Lorcan, I realized that."

What? Now she was the one grabbing for Heath as she lunged forward. "Being imprisoned was a gift?"

"No." His chin lifted. "Losing your memory was. You should thank Lorcan for that. He was merciful to you. If you'd kept those memories, you'd probably be insane."

She was *staring* at someone insane. "Oh, I'll be sure to thank him, all right." She'd thank the bastard by taking his head. That'd really show her gratitude to the jerk.

"Why did he send you here?" Alerac asked as he pulled Jane away from Heath.

Heath's gaze jumped to him. "Because I promised him that I could deliver Jane to him."

She laughed at that.

"It's a promise I'll keep," Heath swore.

"I don't see how," Zoe said as she lifted a brow. Finn stood just behind her. "I mean, considering you're tied to a chair right now, and you look like werewolf chow to me."

Finn growled.

Heath licked his bloody lips. He turned his head, and his eyes found Jane once more. "If you don't go with me, Jane, if you don't go back with me to meet Lorcan, then he's going to hurt someone that you care about."

She frowned at him. "I should believe you because…?"

"Lorcan thinks I'm here to use our friendship."

They didn't have a friendship. They had lies.

"But I saw. I *saw.*"

Good for him. Disgusted, she turned away from him. She didn't want to hear any more of his stories.

"Did you know that you have a brother, Jane?"

Yeah, she did. Jane hesitated. Her gaze slid toward Zoe. The other woman gave an almost imperceptible nod.

"Did you know that he's about to die?"

The guy was bluffing. Jane spun to face him, and her hands fisted on her hips. "I don't think so."

"He has poison in his veins. Poison that Lorcan put there." The hair at his temples was wet with sweat. "Lorcan has the cure to that poison. If you go to him, you can take the cure."

Her heart kicked into her chest. "That's a lie." Another one. Ryan would have mentioned his imminent death, wouldn't he?

Alerac was now staring at Zoe, too. "Bring the vamp in here."

"But—but the sun—"

"I don't care if he's weak, I want him in here."

Zoe nodded, then hurried from the room.

Jane kept staring at Heath. "It's just another lie," she said, sadly. "Another trick. Maybe you were supposed to come here and try to get me to your side, but when you started to heal, you realized that wasn't going to work because we'd all realized that you'd been using my blood—"

"No, dammit, I'm telling you the truth!"

But his truth sounded like lies to her.

Heath exhaled. "It's true, I swear it is. The guy is going to die unless you go meet Lorcan."

She just gazed back at him. *Liar, liar.*

Heath swore and jerked against his ropes. "Don't believe me? Then just *drink* me. Vamps can see memories. As old as you are, you should be able to control the memories you pull up. Lorcan does. He can see anything he wants when he drinks from prey."

"I'm not Lorcan." She might as well be a newborn vamp as far as memory control was concerned. As far as *any* vamp powers were concerned.

"You want your brother to die, *fine*. You can just—"

Ryan burst into the cabin. Zoe was at his side, casting worried glances his way. "What. The. Hell?" Ryan demanded as he advanced toward Alerac.

Then he got a look at the bound man.

Ryan stopped. Frowned. Then shrugged as if seeing a bound human was a typical occurrence for him.

"Is there something you need to tell us?" Alerac asked Ryan.

"Sure. You're an SOB who will never be worthy of my sister?"

Alerac smiled. "Not that." A pause. "Are you dying?"

"Not today," Ryan shot right back.

"The poison's in you!" Heath yelled, straining against the ropes.

Ryan slowly stepped toward the yelling man. "And who might you be?"

"He's the human doctor who found Jane," Alerac told him. "And he's also the man who's been taking her blood."

Ryan's teeth snapped together. "Is he."

"He says you've got poison in you," Alerac continued with a watchful gaze. "And the only way to get a cure? Well, seems Jane has to trade her life for yours."

"I don't want any trade." Flat. Instant.

Jane's breath caught. Wait—he hadn't denied the poison. He'd just said he didn't want a trade. Jane studied him, trying to see past the guard of his handsome face.

"This human works for Lorcan?" Ryan's lips twisted. "He always did like to use his lackeys. He'd get them to do his grunt work, then drain 'em dry. The fools thought they'd get immortality."

Heath's eyes widened.

"All they got was a fast trip to hell."

Heath wasn't struggling any longer.

"Is there poison in your veins?" Jane asked him.

Ryan smiled at her. "That's not your problem. Hell, you don't even *know* me."

No, she didn't have memories of him. "You're my brother." And he'd touched her mind. When he'd sent that message to meet him at the stream, she'd actually felt him in her head. That touch had been strangely comforting. Familiar.

She'd tried to reach out to him again, using that mental link, but Jane had found nothing.

No link.

No comfort.

His face hardened. "You're not going to offer your life for me or for some cure that Lorcan *doesn't* have. I know I've been living on borrowed time. I've known it for nearly two centuries." He rubbed his chin. "It's my own fault. I tried to get him to make me a deal with me. After he took you away, I was willing to do anything, to trade anything, to find you."

Her chest ached.

"Lorcan's witch made me a potion. See, he'd let her keep living because she didn't know exactly where you were imprisoned. He got her to create a special brew. Said that it would connect me to you." His eyes squeezed shut. "I drank it, like a fool, and I got that deeper connection. I could hear you in my head. Crystal fucking clear. You were crying, screaming. Helpless. And those were your real cries. Your body might have frozen, but you were conscious of every moment that passed." He ran a hand over his face. "You were aware and always screaming in your mind. In *my* mind. I could hear you, twenty-four, seven, but I couldn't find you. I couldn't *free* you."

"The potion was poison," Alerac said quietly.

"Son of a bitch," Finn murmured, sounding shaken. "That's twisted."

"That's Lorcan," Ryan said as his eyes opened. "He gets off on playing his games."

Zoe rocked back onto her heels. "I'm surprised you didn't go crazy."

"I did."

Jane shivered. "I-I'm sorry." The thought of him suffering, with her, for all that time...

"I sent you messages with my mind back then," Ryan said, voice soft. Shoulders slumped. "Just like I did when I told you to meet me by the stream."

Alerac tensed.

"Over and over, while you were imprisoned, I'd tell you that everything was going to be all right. That you would be safe. That I'd find you." He swallowed. "But the cries never stopped, and I figured you couldn't hear me."

Jane could only shake her head. She'd sure heard him clearly enough when he told her to meet him at the stream. Maybe she had heard him for all of those other years, too.

Maybe she hadn't.

"Maybe I needed to be closer, in order for you to hear me." Ryan's hands were fisted. "I tried a lot over the last six months." He rolled his shoulders. "You didn't seem to hear me then, either. You didn't seem to hear me until I came to this wolf compound."

I'd had Alerac's blood by then. She frowned. She'd started to get stronger after taking Alerac's blood. Had that made her able to finally connect with her brother's link?

"Doesn't matter." Now Ryan was circling around Heath. "None of that matters now. I took the poison, and there's no going back."

"Why would Lorcan want you dead?" Zoe asked. "You were in his clan!"

"He thought I might one day fight him for power over the clan." A grim smile. "He was right. Though there wasn't exactly much left of our clan." His attention shifted to Alerac. "Not after your wolves tore through our keep."

"What does the poison do?" Zoe edged toward him. "Does it hurt?"

"Every damn minute," Ryan said grimly. "It's like fire in my veins."

Jane swiped away a tear. When had that fallen?

"How long do you have?" Finn wanted to know.

"Now that I've located Keira—Jane," he corrected almost absently, "probably only a day or two more." But he didn't seem to care. Why not? He should care. He was talking about his death too casually. "The potion linked me to her. The witch said it would burn brightest when I found what I sought."

He'd sought her.

"He's going to burn alive," Heath whispered. His gaze swept over them all. "Burn from the inside out. Lorcan thinks he'll die within the next twenty-four hours. But there's a *cure.*"

"He's lying." Ryan whirled away from the human.

Jane stepped into her brother's path. "Drink from him and see." He might be ready to give up and die, but she wasn't ready to let him go.

A faint furrow appeared between Ryan's brows.

"Drink from him. What do we have to lose? Just…see. There could be a chance for you." He'd suffered for so long. Didn't he deserve a chance?

"Why not?" His teeth flashed. "I could go for a bite." He turned back toward Heath. "I'm not going to be gentle."

That was the only warning Heath had. Ryan grabbed for the man, twisted his head to the side, and shoved his fangs into Heath's throat.

Jane's own throat burned. Liam had done that to her. He'd wrenched her head to the side—

"Jane."

Alerac. His voice. His hand on her arm.

She blinked. When had he moved so close to her?

"It's okay," he told her. His voice was strong and certain. She glanced away from Alerac and back to her brother.

Ryan had freed Heath. "Fuck me." There was shock in his voice. Ryan swiped a hand over his lips, wiping away the blood. *"There is a cure."*

Relief made her a little dizzy. There was a cure, and it looked like they had about twenty-four hours to find it.

***

"They'll come for the cure," Lorcan said as he glanced over his shoulder. His witch stood there, pressing her back into the corner. For a being so powerful, she was also incredibly weak.

Breakable.

The marks on her neck were just starting to heal.

It was so hard to find good witches these days.

"They'll come, and I'll kill them." Simple. He'd deliberately let Heath learn of the cure. Every move that he'd made had been deliberate.

If Heath hadn't been killed on sight at the werewolf compound, then either Ryan or Keira would drink from the human. They would look into his memories.

That was the way of the vampire.

When they took his blood, they'd learn of the cure. They'd learn of Lorcan's hiding spot in the mountains.

They'd plan an attack.

Alerac would follow his bread crumbs so perfectly. So foolishly.

You destroyed my clan. Now it's my turn to destroy your pack.

Everything was falling into place. Every fucking thing.

He crooked his finger toward the witch.

When she flinched, he smiled. "Come now, my dear, it's almost time for you to do your part."

She had a role to play, just as he did. Only once his lovely witch had done his bidding, then he'd kill her.

She was incredibly weak, and he despised weakness. *It would soon be time for a new model.*

***

"He's waiting on the other side of the mountain, in a blue house just past the bridge." Ryan's voice was flat. "I saw the house in the human's mind. Lorcan is there."

"It's a trap." Alerac knew this. They all had to know this. "We aren't trading Jane." That plan was pure shit.

Jane stood near the fireplace. No fire burned. She stared at the empty hearth. "I don't understand. If he wanted me dead, if he wanted me at all, why didn't he come for me himself when I was free? Why wait six months? Why start the attacks now?"

Alerac wanted to know the answers to those questions, too. At first, he'd thought that he'd gotten lucky. That he'd found Jane first.

Lucky hadn't been in the equation.

Lorcan was playing them.

"Lorcan is a tricky bastard. He's always manipulating, playing his games." Ryan was close to Jane's side. "I don't know why—"

"There wasn't anything special in her blood," Heath muttered.

Alerac frowned at him. "A vampire's blood, by its very nature, is fucking special." It had certainly healed the human.

But Heath shook his head. He was sweating, but no longer bleeding. Fear oozed from the man's pores. Probably because he realized that he wouldn't be living much longer. Not much longer at all. "Liam had me comparing her blood to other vamps. He was—he was looking for something in her blood. Some kind of power that wasn't there. He kept saying that it *should* be there."

Liam knew that Alerac had grown stronger after taking Jane's blood. That he'd transformed into something that was both werewolf and vampire.

Liam had taken the blood of other vampires so that his life could be extended. So that he could fight at Alerac's side. But he'd never gotten the power boost that Alerac had received. Never transformed into a hybrid creature.

Only Alerac had done that — with the aid of Jane's blood.

"I think Liam and Lorcan both want to know how you changed me." Alerac made sure that his voice carried easily across the room. "Hell, maybe Lorcan even held back on making contact with you because he wanted me to find you first. He probably even wanted us to mate, so that he could see the changes." Was that why the guy hadn't directly come at them yet? He was waiting, watching?

Her breath whispered out. "Changes?"

"The sun isn't hurting you anymore. You aren't weak, and you *should* be weak during the day."

Her lashes lowered.

"Maybe Lorcan wanted you to spend time with me because he wanted —" Alerac broke off. *He wanted us to mate. To fuck. To bond.* "When you came from your imprisonment, you weren't linked to me." Those words were so hard to utter, but they were true. He'd been tied to her, body and soul, for two centuries.

She'd shared no such tie with him.

So Lorcan had tried to reset the bond.

In order to see the power in her blood? "We're Lorcan's experiment," Alerac said. "And he wants us—both of us—so he can figure out how to get the same power for himself."

Alerac's attraction to Jane had been undeniable, too consuming, and it was being used against him now.

"I don't have much time left," Ryan said, voice grim. "But I'm going to make the most of that time. I'll do my best to take him out."

Alerac shook his head. "You've tried before. That didn't work—"

"I couldn't kill him for the same reason you couldn't—he knew where Jane was! If he'd died, we might never have seen her again." His gaze cut to Jane. "When the screams stopped, I thought for sure you were dead."

Pain flashed in her eyes.

Ryan backed toward the door. "You aren't trading for me. You aren't trading yourself for anyone, ever again." He pointed toward Alerac. "Keep her safe, wolf. If you don't, I'll come back and haunt your ass."

Then he yanked open the door, and the fool ran right out in the sunlight.

"Ryan!" Jane tried to go after him. Not happening. Alerac wrapped his forearm around her stomach and pulled her back against him. "Dammit, let me go!"

No.

"Zoe!" He trusted her. *As I trusted Liam.* His back teeth ground together. "Follow him and make sure he doesn't get himself killed."

Zoe was already running through the door.

"Finn."

Finn jerked to attention.

"Has anyone found Liam's tracks?" The guy was good at covering himself. He should be good. Alerac had taught him well.

Finn shook his head. "It's like he just vanished."

But he hadn't. Liam would be turning up again. Like Lorcan, he was after the power that could come from Jane.

And like Lorcan, he wasn't getting her.

Two enemies after me. Time to even up the odds a bit.

"Make sure the human doesn't leave," he ordered Finn.

Jane turned in his grasp. "You're going after Lorcan."

Yes. Ryan would be his distraction. While Lorcan and his lackeys were fighting Ryan, Alerac would engage his own attack. "I'll take men with me. The bastard won't live to see another sunset."

Alerac couldn't wait to rip him apart.

"If you go, then I go." Jane was adamant.

Alerac opened his mouth to argue.

"If I took your punishment, then don't you think you owe this to me?" Her words vibrated with intensity. "Two hundred years. I won't stand on the sidelines anymore. I won't keep hiding. I *can't.*"

Alerac closed his mouth because he had no words.

"Your pack backs us, my brother fights, you fight." Her shoulders straightened. "I fight, too."

He didn't want her anywhere near Lorcan.

"I won't be shut out. I've lost my past, but I'm not losing my future."

"You will!" This came from Heath. "He'll kill you, Jane! Don't do this! He's going to—"

"Gag him," Jane snapped to Finn.

A grin curling his lips, Finn moved to obey. Soon all Heath could do was grunt.

"I'm a vampire. And, thanks to you, I'm also more." She held Alerac's gaze. "Let's see just how much power we have together. Let's see if we can make Lorcan fear *us* this time."

This wasn't the scared woman who'd run from him when he first saw her in Wylee's bar. It wasn't even the delicate vampire princess who'd first stolen into his heart on a long ago night in Ireland.

This woman…determination burned in her eyes. Fury hardened her muscles.

She was the most beautiful thing he'd ever seen.

Alerac nodded. "We will make him fear."

And beg.

And…*die.*

***

Liam watched them leave. Alerac took most of his men with him. He took Jane.

The alpha made sure to keep her right at his side.

The storm had helped Liam. It had covered his scent. Hid his tracks.

He'd learned a few other ways to hide his scent over the years, even from someone with senses as powerful as Alerac's.

The motorcycles roared away.

The sun hadn't weakened Jane.

It looked like she was changing, too.

He waited until the growl of the motorcycles died away. He'd been watching the main house carefully. He'd seen the activity there.

The familiar human who'd been dragged inside.

The human who hadn't come out. He was sure that Heath had told them all of Liam's secrets.

Heath would pay for that.

Liam surveyed the area. Only a few wolves remained. Alerac must think he'd need his pack's support in the coming battle, but the alpha should have planned better.

He should have left more of a defense at home.

If you didn't protect what you valued, then you only had yourself to blame when it was destroyed.

Liam carefully worked his way to the main house, never making a sound, barely breathing.

Then he slipped in through a back window. He knew every inch of that house. Knew which boards would squeak beneath his feet. Which doors would creak when he opened them.

There were no squeaks. No creaks.

He saw the human. Bound. A gag in his mouth. Heath's eyes widened when he caught sight of Liam. The human started to jerk and twist, and his gaze darted behind Liam's form.

Ah, a warning. Interesting.

He spun around just as Finn charged at him.

But poor Finn never had a chance. He wasn't immortal. He hadn't been gorging on vampire blood for two lifetimes.

Liam drove his hand into Finn's chest. Then he pulled out the werewolf's heart.

When Finn fell to the floor, Liam was smiling.

The human whimpered behind his gag.

Liam dropped the heart. He turned back to his new prey. "Well, well…I guess we meet again." There was dried blood on Heath's neck and shirt. Someone had been drinking from him.

Taking his memoires?

Liam already had enough memories in his head. Memories that seemed to tear him apart. Memories from the vampires. From their countless attacks. Again and again. He didn't even dream anymore—he just saw the memories.

Endlessly.

Sometimes, he wasn't sure if those memories belonged to the vampires he'd killed—*or to me.*

His fingers tightened on Heath's throat. "You were supposed to be working with me. That was why I paid you so much."

Tears filled the man's eyes. He was muttering frantically behind his gag. Liam narrowed his eyes. "If you try to scream, I'll rip out your throat."

A desperate nod.

Liam jerked out the gag.

"Pl…please…" Heath wheezed. "I can still help you."

And he would. "Where are they?"

"They went…after Lorcan."

A foolish move. "Alerac actually took Jane to him?" After all he'd done to keep her out of the vamp's reach?

"Her brother is d-dying. Lorcan has a cure."

Her brother. The prick Ryan. *How many times did I say he needed to lose his head?* But Alerac hadn't listened to him. Alerac never listened to him.

"Where is Lorcan?"

"Southside of the mountain. In the blue house, the one with the windows boarded up."

How like a vamp to hide behind boarded windows, cowering from the sun.

"Is that all you've got?" Liam murmured.

"I-I can help—"

Liam snapped Heath's neck. "No, you can die." Because the human had failed him too many times already.

The he glanced around the cabin. He knew what this place was. Alerac's home for *her*. Alerac thought to offer the princess a perfect sanctuary.

They wouldn't have that.

He'd destroy them—he'd destroy everything.

CHAPTER TEN

The sun blazed down on them as Alerac and Jane crept toward the blue house. Heavy boards covered the windows. There were no cars outside the structure, no vehicles of any sort.

The pack had left their motorcycles a few miles away. They hadn't wanted to alert Lorcan to their approach. Now they closed in on the house, surrounding it from all sides.

"Where's Ryan?" Jane whispered as she edged closer to Alerac. She hadn't caught sight of Ryan or Zoe.

Alerac's nostrils flared, as if he were pulling in her brother's scent. "Heading to the right. Dammit, he's getting too close to the house. He needs to wait!"

Ryan wasn't going to wait for anyone.

"How many are in the house?" Jane asked. "Can you hear them?"

"I count five." His gaze locked on the front door. But then he frowned. "Five, but I smell…" His eyes widened. "*Back!*" Alerac roared.

He grabbed Jane and began running with her.

Just as the blue house exploded.

The blast lifted Jane and Alerac both into the air. It tossed them, and then they slammed down into the hard earth.

She glanced back at the house — only there was no house. Just flames.

"Ryan?" Jane whispered her brother's name.

Zoe ran from the flames. Her clothes were smoking. Blood dripped from a gash on her forehead.

"Ryan?" Jane jumped to her feet. Alerac tried to stop her, but she wasn't in the mood to be stopped. "*Ryan!*"

Zoe grabbed her hands. "I'm sorry. I tried to pull him back — "

No, no, this couldn't happen. They'd gone there to save Ryan.

She tried desperately to use the mental link that was supposed to be between them.

But Jane's mind touched nothing.

Then she heard laughter. Sick, twisted laughter that seemed to come from the very flames.

The red and orange flames stretched into the sky. They burned white-hot. She could feel the lance of that heat against her skin.

She yanked free of Zoe's hold and followed that laughter. It wasn't coming *from* the flames, but from the woods that were behind the house.

Lorcan stood there. Arms crossed over his chest. A dead werewolf at his feet. And a pale, scared blond woman at his side.

Though the sun was out, Lorcan certainly didn't look weak, not in any way.

"*Lorcan.*" Alerac snarled his name with fury and hate.

Jane could only stare at him. This man — with his perfect looks, his too pale skin, and his icy eyes — he was the one who'd wreaked havoc on her life for so very long.

Alerac charged toward him.

"Make the wolf hurt," Lorcan ordered.

The blond woman lifted her hand. Then she clenched her fingers into a fist. Alerac fell down, howling as he clawed at his chest.

Alerac's men — those still alive — were gathering around them. She could hear bones snapping, and Jane knew they were shifting in preparation for an attack.

The blonde's gaze found Jane's. *I'm sorry.* The woman mouthed the words.

"Don't be," Jane shouted right back. "Because Lorcan is going to die!"

She wasn't going to let Alerac be in pain. She wasn't just going to *stand* there. Jane leapt forward, feeling her own claws break from her fingertips even as her fangs burned in her mouth.

For his crimes, Lorcan would die. And as for the blonde — *you're his witch, aren't you?* — she'd be joining the vampire in hell.

Lorcan smiled at her. "Want me? Then come get me."

She *was*.

She raced toward him, going faster, faster, faster —

And he was waiting. Not even trying to back away. Grinning and waiting for her attack.

The witch still had her hand clenched into a fist. Jane didn't know what kind of spell the woman was working, but — *it ends.*

At the last second, right before Jane would have collided with Lorcan, she whirled and took that witch down.

Because I won't let Alerac suffer.

Jane drove her claws into the woman's chest. The blond screamed, and her hands opened as she tried to fight Jane.

"You don't hurt him," Jane said as she shoved the woman back into the woods. "No one does."

Then she turned on Lorcan.

That smile was still in place on his face. *Wrong expression, jerk.* Didn't he realize this was when he was supposed to be afraid?

There was no more snapping of bones behind her. No more howls. A fast and frantic glance showed her that the wolves had shifted, and they stalked forward quickly, surrounding Lorcan.

No escape.

Alerac rose from the ground. His breath heaved out as he lunged forward and put himself right next to Jane.

This was it. The end.

So why wasn't Lorcan afraid?

"You think you're going to take my head?" Lorcan shook the head in question. "You do underestimate me."

"Your death has been a long time coming," Alerac told him. "So let's not wait any more."

His claws flew up and went right for Lorcan's throat.

There was still no fear in Lorcan's eyes.

Alerac sliced his claws across Lorcan's neck.

And Jane fell to the ground. Blood poured from *her* neck, from a wound that she shouldn't have. From a wound that matched Lorcan's.

Lorcan's throat was bleeding, but he was still on his feet, and his eyes gleamed with an unholy light.

"Jane? *Jane!*" Alerac rushed to her.

She tried to put her hand over her neck, to stop the flow of blood.

"Kill him!" Alerac ordered his men. "Do it, *now!*"

The wolves leapt forward to attack.

One wolf sank his teeth into Lorcan's forearm.

Jane screamed as phantom teeth tore into her arm.

"What the hell…?" Alerac stared at her wound with desperate eyes. Then he whirled toward the swarming wolves.

Phantom teeth sank into her leg. Tore muscles.

"*Stop! Stop the attack!*" Alerac bellowed.

The wolves froze.

Jane couldn't get off the ground. Blood soaked her.

Lorcan was on the ground, too. Covered in just as much blood. His head was turned toward Jane. He was…smiling. Still.

"I've linked us," he said, the words little more than a whisper, yet she heard him clearly. "You don't remember, but you accepted the bond. You won't ever be his, not really, because you are mine. Body and soul, *forever.*"

No, no, this wasn't right.

"My pain…is yours. Your life…is mine."

She wanted to deny it, but Jane couldn't. Not when her injuries were a perfect match to his.

"Go get that witch!" Alerac pointed to the woods.

She'd tossed the witch that way, hadn't she?

Darkness thickened around Jane.

"If your wolf, kills…me. Then he kills you…too."

Sick bastard.

She turned her head. Saw the flames, still shooting into the sky. Her brother had gone into those flames.

I didn't get to know him.

Her heart ached.

"Jane, it's going to be all right." Alerac was before her. He'd slit his lower arm, and he pushed the blood offering toward her lips. "Just drink from me."

She was hurt badly, she knew it. The wounds should have killed her — and Lorcan.

Without Alerac's blood, she would die right there on the ground. So Jane drank. And as she drank, Alerac's powerful blood healed her.

It also healed Lorcan.

Soon he was on his feet, no wounds on his body. Healed too fast, from blood that he'd never tasted.

"Amazing, isn't it?" Lorcan murmured. "How some bonds can cut through flesh and be buried in the blood? And that is our bond. Through blood and pain…until death."

Two wolves broke from the woods. The blonde woman was in front of them. She was bleeding, stumbling, but she didn't look in immediate danger of dying.

Zoe hurried toward the witch. "You try a spell on me, and I'll knock your ass out."

The blonde's head was bowed. "You are already under one spell. Mine will not weaken you anymore than you are—"

"Did you just say I'm weak?" Zoe leapt for her.

"Don't kill her, Zoe. I need the witch alive." Alerac's voice. Flat. Alerac pulled Jane to her feet, then he wrapped his arm around her. Wolves still circled Lorcan, trapping him with their bodies. "You sonofabitch, you think you've won, don't you?"

Lorcan smirked. "Unless you're planning to kill the vampiress there, then, yes, I have." He rubbed at his neck, at the wound that wasn't there any longer. "You see, you can't kill me—not fucking ever—not if you want the one you call Jane to keep walking on this earth with you."

How had he done it? *How?*

Magic, witchcraft, terrified Jane.

And Lorcan pissed her off. "You killed my brother."

A shrug. "He was going to die anyway. The poison had eaten up his insides, and it was starting to play with his mind." Lorcan tapped his forehead. "The mind is the weakest part, you know. Once it breaks, there's no saving the body. Or the soul."

"You don't have a soul," she whispered.

"And you don't have a life," he fired back, "not without me."

Alerac's body felt like stone against hers. She knew he wanted Lorcan's head. But if he attacked Lorcan, then Alerac would hurt her.

"You had men in that house," she said, her mind struggling desperately to find a way out of this nightmare.

"I had bait in that house. They were expendable."

So cold. Callous.

"I also have men coming from the woods now. I'd say, Alerac, that you have about one minute to get your pack to safety, and then the silver bullets will start flying." Lorcan's lips twisted. "Ah, didn't I tell you? I planned for that stupid human to tell you my location — and to tell you about the so-called cure for Ryan. I needed you here. I needed you to bring me Jane."

And they had.

"There was no cure," she said, voice leaden.

"Sure there was," Lorcan told her, frowning. "Death is the cure. It always is."

What?

"Now leave Jane here with me, and run while you can."

Alerac's head tilted toward the woods. "I don't smell them."

"I've cloaked their scents. A little trick I learned from a voodoo priestess in Africa."

Alerac's teeth snapped together. "Don't smell 'em, but I hear 'em — *attack!*"

The wolves jumped into motion, even as the thunder of gunfire erupted. Bullets slammed the two wolves who were next to the witch. They howled in pain, and their coats thickened with blood.

The witch sank to the ground, her hands going over her head.

Then a bullet drove into her shoulder.

More bullets. More cries. More blood.

"Enough!" Alerac roared. Then he was hurtling forward. Transforming, shifting, and running toward the woods.

He had to protect his pack.

She had to help him.

Jane ran after him. She spared one final glare for Lorcan.

"I'll see you again!" he called out.

She chased her werewolf into the woods.

A bullet grazed her arm. *I hope you feel that, Lorcan.*

Then a man in black charged at her.

She grabbed the gun right out of his hands. With a quick twist, Jane broke those hands. Then she sank her teeth into the guy's throat.

Alerac's wolf was growling. Attacking. Taking down men left and right.

And they were just men — not vampires. Men. Mortal men who were in over their heads.

They'd chosen the wrong side in this fight.

Another bullet hit Jane in the back. She dropped her prey. He wasn't a threat any longer. Not dead, but not about to fight back.

She spun on the new attacker. The bloodlust within her was rising as it never had before.

The man who'd just shot her was taking aim at Alerac now.

No.

She rushed toward him. Before he could fire, her teeth were in his neck.

***

The bastard called Lorcan was getting away. Zoe chased after him, trying to dodge the bullets that were still flying. Silver. She *hated* silver.

What werewolf didn't?

Lorcan was rushing into a dilapidated storage building that was about thirty yards away from the remains of the burning house.

She heard the growl of an engine.

No.

When a truck burst from the side of that storage building moments later, Zoe jumped in its path. She had to stop him.

Lorcan was behind the wheel. Smiling at her. He reeved that engine and the vehicle zoomed right at her.

Wait for it. Wait for it. She could do this. She could —

Something slammed into Zoe. She went flying, and when she hit the ground again, she found herself staring up at —

A dead man.

Ryan glared down at her. Blisters covered his face and neck, and his skin seemed to be white-hot where it touched her. She could actually feel the scorch on her body.

"Got a death wish?" Ryan asked.

"No, that's you." She was stronger than she looked. So much stronger. She could have stopped that truck.

Maybe.

Now she pushed him aside. Her stomach was knotting. Her heart racing, and she was happy — *no, couldn't be happy, just relieved, for Jane's sake* — that Ryan was still alive.

Though she didn't even know how the hell he was walking around. Vamps and fire were supposed to be a deadly combination.

Hell, with that much fire, it should have meant death for anyone.

Zoe jumped to her feet. The truck was vanishing down the road. She started to chase it.

"Don't. We have something more valuable here." Ryan grabbed her hands.

Again, his touch seemed to scorch her.

He pointed to the bloody, cowering witch. "Consider her our GPS device."

The gunfire stopped. Wolves shifted into human form, then transformed almost instantly back into beasts. They were trying to push the silver from their bodies. Trying to heal.

She glanced around, frantic, but only counted one dead — the poor wolf that Lorcan had killed when the house exploded.

Her shoulders sagged. She'd buried too many of her pack mates over the years.

Too many.

Ryan marched toward the witch. He caught the blonde's arm and jerked her upright.

Her blood soaked her shirt.

"Don't!" The blonde cried. "I didn't want to help him! I didn't have a choice."

"Bullshit," Ryan tossed right back at her. "We all have choices. Right now, my choice is — do I let you talk or do I just pick a vein and find the real truth through your blood?"

The vampire was fierce. Zoe had always found tough guys to be a turn-on.

Except when they were about to drink blood. Then…*not so much.*

Before Ryan could make his choice, Jane appeared, bursting from the woods. She was covered in blood, sporting some rather vicious claws, and her fangs were most definitely out.

This didn't look at all like the scared, lost woman that had first arrived at the werewolf compound with Alerac.

Jane looked like she could kick serious ass — and she just had.

A dark wolf walked at her side. His body was massive, and his shining green gaze promised hell.

Jane put her hand on his head, stroking him.

Then Jane saw Ryan. She stopped. Shook her head. "R-Ryan?" In the next instant, she was running toward the vampire. Jane through her body against his and held on, tight.

The witch didn't move.

Lucky girl, she'd just been spared a drinking. For the moment, anyway.

But Zoe knew that reprieve wouldn't last forever. In her experience, nothing lasted forever.

Not even vampires.

***

Alerac knew something was wrong the instant that he stepped back onto his land.

The scent of blood was too heavy. Too fresh.

He rushed toward the main house. "Finn!" He threw open the door. Ran into the great-room.

Finn's body was on the floor. The human — with his neck twisted — hung in his binds. The human's chest had been clawed open.

"No!" Zoe shoved past them and ran to Finn. She fell to her knees beside him. "No, Finn!"

Fuck. Finn and Zoe had come to Alerac's pack together. Not linked by blood, but by friendship. A deep and abiding friendship formed as abandoned children tossed from home to home in a foster care system that sure as hell hadn't been made for their kind.

No one had understood their rage. Their bloodlust. And when puberty hit and the beast surged for power—the humans had tossed both Finn and Zoe into a psych ward, convinced they were going mad.

Alerac had found them. He'd gotten them out.

"Finn, don't leave me," Zoe begged.

He was already gone.

Jane crossed toward Zoe. She hesitated, then put her hand on Zoe's shoulder.

Ryan dragged the witch over the threshold. His gaze immediately found Zoe. Tears tracked endlessly down her cheeks. He swore and hauled the witch to Zoe's side. "He...matters to you?"

Zoe glanced up, staring at him as if he were crazy.

"Hell, of course, he matters." Ryan expelled a rough breath. Then he shook the witch. "Bring him back."

Ryan was insane. Not surprising, really. Alerac had long suspected that he was.

"Ryan," Jane began, voice uncertain, "this can't—"

"He's not human, right?"

"His *heart* is gone," Jane snapped to her brother. "He can't come back!"

Ryan frowned, and shook his head. "But she wants him back." He touched his temple. "Bring him back."

Yes, definitely insane.

"I can't," the witch whispered. "He's not here anymore."

A choked sob came from Zoe.

The witch glanced at Alerac. "Please, let me go."

Not likely. He still remembered what had happened when the witch used her magic on him. He'd felt as if someone were cutting out *his* heart.

But Zoe couldn't keep holding Finn. Alerac motioned through the open doorway, at the two werewolves who were watching in shocked silence. "Take care of Finn. Bury the human."

They nodded.

Zoe tightened her hold on him. "You can't do this! You can't—" But then she stopped. She inhaled. Stared down at Finn with watery eyes. "I thought it was Lorcan. That he'd done this."

So had Alerac. At first.

"Liam?" Zoe whispered as she inhaled. Then she screamed, "*Liam!*"

Yes, Alerac had caught his scent, too. Liam had come back, and he'd hunted right in Alerac's home.

Was the bastard still close?

Alerac glanced back through the open door. *You are, aren't you?* "Keep the witch here," Alerac told Ryan. "I'm hunting." He couldn't kill Lorcan, not yet, but Liam was another matter. Liam had earned the death he had coming his way.

He'd betrayed the pack, turned on his own kind.

He would die.

Alerac pointed to the witch. "Find a way to break the spell that links Jane and Lorcan."

"I can't—"

"Find it, or you die. Because you're no fuckin' use to me otherwise." Then his stare cut to Jane.

Jane.

It almost hurt to look at her. Because—*I nearly killed her.* He hadn't realized it. Had never suspected that Lorcan had somehow linked their life forces.

If he'd severed Lorcan's head from his body, Jane would have died, too. In an instant.

When he'd whirled and seen the blood flowing down her neck, horror had filled him. He hadn't been able to get to her fast enough. Hadn't been able to heal her soon enough.

He wanted to cross the room and take her into his arms.

But his job was to protect. To protect Jane. To protect the pack. So far, he'd failed at that job.

No longer.

No other wolves would die by Liam's hand. Liam had been his best friend. His closest confidant for two hundred years. It was only fitting that Alerac be the one to end him.

Fitting? No, maybe just twisted.

But it had to be done.

"Sever the tie between them," Alerac commanded the witch. He couldn't even look at Finn's body then.

He headed back outside, into the too bright sunlight.

"Alerac!"

Jane. She'd rushed toward him so quickly. "Let me come with you."

There were some battles that he had to fight on his own. "Figure out a way to save your brother. Maybe the cure wasn't total bull."

Then he faced the sun. He inhaled the scents. And followed the trail that he knew Liam had deliberately left for him.

***

Jane grabbed the witch and pretty much dragged the woman upstairs. Zoe and Ryan followed her, though Zoe just looked shattered.

I've looked that way before.

Jane pushed the witch into the bedroom on the right. "Tell me your name."

"M-Mina."

Jane frowned at her, that name was familiar. She'd seen a movie, during her vampire research and—

"At least, that's what he called me." Mina's voice was softer now. "I've been with him since I was five. I don't really know…I don't remember what I was called before that."

"Dracula's freaking bride." Ryan sounded disgusted. "Guess it makes sense that he'd call you that. Asshole probably thinks that it's funny."

Mina's head whipped up. "I'm not his bride." Her index finger pointed to Jane. "She's his bride."

The hell she was. "You're a witch," Jane said. Stating the obvious, right?

But Mina still nodded.

"Tell me about the poison in my brother."

"I-I didn't craft that poison."

"Right, of course you didn't," the disgusted snap came from Ryan. Zoe stared at them all, her hands wrapped around her stomach. Ryan continued, "Because you weren't Lorcan's flavor of choice back then. That was another witch. He killed her after she locked my sister in her prison with magic and poisoned me." He braced his legs apart as he stared at Mina. "But every poison has a cure, right?"

A timid nod.

"What cures me?"

Mina's gaze darted to Zoe.

Ryan's eyes narrowed. "What. Cures. Me?"

Mina swiped away a tear that had slid down her cheek. "I read the old book that Shonna left behind."

Shonna. The name meant nothing to Jane. Big surprise.

"Shonna was his witch back in the day," Ryan explained. Had he read her mind, used their link to see what she was thinking? Or had he just guessed?

"The book said that the poison could be purged if you took the blood of a caged beast." Mina spoke quickly. "She said the beast had to be dormant, locked, and your poison would destroy that beast even as you were healed."

Ryan had turned to stare at Zoe. "Fuck me."

Jane's gaze darted between them.

Zoe laughed. "It's me? You think I'm your cure?" Her eyes were on the floor, not on Ryan. "I'm a curse. Not a cure. Trust me."

"Don't worry," Ryan told her, voice thick. "I'm not about to *destroy* you." He turned his glare back on the witch. "Think of another way."

Jane heard a howl then, seeming to echo off the mountain. She headed toward the window. Stared out. She didn't see Alerac, but she knew that he was out there. Hunting.

Preparing to kill the closest thing that he had to a brother.

"I shouldn't have let him go alone." He'd been so determined. She'd been—

Lost. Desperate. Because she'd wanted to find a way to sever her tie to Lorcan. She still needed to find a way to be free, but…

Another howl sounded. That howl was harder. Wilder.

Not Alerac's. She knew his cry. Could recognize it on an instinctive level.

"Liam is luring Alerac to him," Zoe murmured.

Yes, he was.

And she was supposed to wait there? Just wait and see who survived this battle?

No.

She spun back to face the witch. "How did Lorcan convince you to stay with him? To help him for all this time?"

Mina's lips trembled. "I had no one else. He killed my parents when I was a child. He took my blood, over and over again. He kept me weak. So weak."

She was weak right then. Too thin. Too frail. Trembling as she stood there.

"I'm sorry," Ryan said.

The witch blinked.

"But I'm going to need your blood, too." In an instant, he was at the witch's side. He'd grabbed her hand and lifted her wrist to his mouth. "I don't have time to find out if you're lying or not. I need to know how to live, and I need to know how to keep my sister alive."

He sank his fangs into her wrist.

***

The wolf stalked carefully over the stream. Jane's blood had covered the rocks in this stream. She'd been attacked, right here, when she should have been safe on his land.

Rage twisted within Alerac.

Liam's scent was stronger here, leading him deeper into the woods.

After your attack on Finn, you knew I'd be the one to hunt you.

Liam was sure leaving him a clear path to follow.

Liam had never challenged him for alpha status. He'd always stood at Alerac's side.

Until now.

Now the challenge was undeniable.

Alerac's head lowered over the water. He eased away from the stream. Liam's scent went back to the north. Higher up the mountain.

His head lifted. Alerac looked behind him. He could just see the roof of his home.

A wolf howled from the woods.

A battle waited.

***

Mina gasped when Ryan's teeth sank into her skin. Zoe surged forward.

But Ryan was already drinking. Mina's eyes had gone wide and glassy, and she stood stock-still, as if caught in a nightmare.

If Lorcan had been feeding on her for years, this probably was a nightmare for her.

"Stop, Ryan," Jane demanded.

He didn't.

So she made him. "Stop!" Jane shoved him away.

He swiped the blood away from his mouth and frowned at her.

"Do you just drink from everyone?" Zoe snapped. "Control yourself!"

Jane touched Mina's shoulder. "That's not the way."

"Are you *kidding* me?" Ryan's voice was shocked. "She's his witch. She's not going to help us! We have to make her reveal what she knows."

Mina's stare was still lost. No, blank.

"It's okay," Jane said softly as she tried to reassure the other woman.

"The hell it is," Ryan fired right back. "I'm dying, and you're somehow blood linked to a sadistic SOB who won't stop until he sees your werewolf cold in the ground. How is that 'okay' in any way?"

Mina's lashes lowered. "I'm sorry that I made your werewolf hurt."

She'd said that before. No, she'd mouthed the words as she attacked Alerac. "What did you do to him?"

"Squeezed his heart, cut it, with my magic."

Ryan whistled. "Using black magic. But else would Lorcan's witch use?"

Mina shook her head. "I wasn't always like this." Then her eyes were on Jane. "I don't think I was, but I can't really be sure."

Jane swallowed. "We're not going to hurt you."

Mina risked a glance at Ryan.

"He just wants to live," Jane told her, trying to make Mina understand. "Is that so wrong?"

"I-I told him how…the only cure I know."

Biting a caged beast. One that he'd in turn destroy.

Mina shook her head as her eyes flickered toward Zoe. "It's not like you can even shift, anyway. Why not let the beast go in order to save him?"

Zoe's lips parted in shock.

Then Mina was staring back at Jane. "If I tell you what you need to know, will you let me go?"

"Yes," Jane said at once.

Even as Ryan bellowed, "No!"

Mina nodded. "It's easy, really." But her smile was sad. "If you want to sever the link with Lorcan, you just have to die."

Ryan swore.

"The link he created with you endures until death. Your blood. Your vow. There is no way to break it." Sadness whispered in Mina's words. "You will be linked to him, you will share his pain as you share his life. Until death," she said again, voice even softer.

This information was *not* helping.

"Shonna wrote about the bond. It was the last notation in her book." Mina's smile was sad. "A witch's spell book is supposed to be sacred."

"Why did Lorcan keep her book around?" Jane was surprised that Lorcan hadn't destroyed the spell book when he'd killed Shonna.

"Because he wanted to make sure those spells lasted. If any of that magic started to weaken, he just made sure the new witch—"

Yeah, currently Mina was that new witch.

" —did her best to reinforce the magic." Mina exhaled on a long sigh. "I'm telling you the truth here. If you want your wolf to be free, if you want Lorcan to die, then *you* must die."

That solution sucked.

"Now I get to go." Mina hurried for the door.

Ryan blocked her path.

"I don't know any more than that!" Mina said, voice high and scared and angry. "Please! Let me go!"

"No." He shook his head. "You won't—"

Zoe curled her fingers around his arm, stopping his angry words. "Did you see the scars on her neck?" Zoe's words were quiet. "The scars that go up her arms? That probably cover her entire body?"

Jane had seen the scars. Bite marks. They'd pushed compassion through her. "Let her go," Jane said, her voice as soft as Zoe's. "She's told us all that she can." Jane believed that.

Zoe nodded. It seemed the werewolf believed Mina, too.

But still Ryan hesitated. His gaze had softened, but he wasn't moving. "We need to know where Lorcan went."

"You don't have to go find him." Mina's smile was bitter. "He'll be back here, the moment he thinks you're at your weakest."

"Sounds like him," Ryan muttered. Then he stepped aside.

Mina's shoulders slumped. "Thank you."

She skirted out of the room. Jane followed her. She wanted to make sure the wolves below knew that the witch was clear.

Only…

There were no wolves below. There should have been. They should have been guarding the house.

Where are they?

Mina was running down the stairs.

Jane just jumped right over the bannister and hit the bottom floor, her knees barely buckling. The enhanced power that she'd gotten after taking Alerac's blood was sure a nice bonus.

Finn's body was gone. So was Heath's.

Jane tilted her head. She'd been distracted upstairs and hadn't noticed the silence. So complete. Too complete.

Mina yanked open the house's front door.

Some of Alerac's packmates should have been out there, protecting that door.

The men were on the ground, not moving.

"Wh-what's happening?" Mina's voice shook as she turned to glance back at Jane.

"Get away from the door!" Jane screamed as she lunged for the witch.

But it was too late. Because even as Jane rushed toward Mina, she saw Liam appear behind the witch. His claws drove right into Mina's back.

"*No!*" Jane screamed.

Mina's eyes were on hers. Shocked. Pain-filled. Terrified.

Those eyes were on Jane, and the life was slowly bleeding away from them, even as Mina's blood soaked her clothing once more.

Then Liam tossed Mina aside, as if she were of no more consequence than garbage. To him, she probably was. He didn't know anything about Mina or her pain, and he didn't care.

Liam filled the doorway.

Footsteps thundered from overhead. Ryan. Zoe. Rushing down in response to Jane's scream.

"I knew he'd leave you...leave you waiting for me." Liam leapt toward her.

She didn't back away from him. Her own claws ripped free, and she attacked him. They collided in a tangle of limbs and claws.

"Get away from her!" Ryan's yell.

Liam wasn't getting away from her. She raked her claws over his stomach. This man—he thought to hurt her Alerac? Thought to destroy the pack? "You were his friend!"

"I was his fucking shadow," Liam snarled right back. "No more."

"You're right." That booming voice was Alerac's. And he was—he was standing right behind Liam. "No more."

Liam whirled to confront him. But even as he turned, shoving Jane to the side, Alerac was attacking. Alerac's claws sank into Liam's chest.

"You're not the only one who knows how to disguise his scent," Alerac told him as he sank his claws even deeper in Liam's chest.

Liam cried out.

But Alerac wasn't showing mercy. Alerac was taking Liam's heart. Just as Liam had taken Finn's heart. Part of Jane wanted to look away from the horrible sight, but she couldn't. She couldn't move at all.

Ryan pushed into her back. Zoe gasped.

"You were like a brother to me," Alerac told Liam, voice thundering. *"Why? Why betray me?"*

Liam shoved his hand, no, his claws—right over Alerac's chest.

"No!" Now Jane was moving. Because she was desperate. She grabbed Liam, but couldn't pull him away from Alerac. The werewolf was too strong. If she couldn't get him to break free, then both werewolves might die.

Not happening.

Jane sank her teeth into Liam's neck. Liam jerked his hand back as he tried to attack her.

And images, dozens of them, immediately swam through her mind.

Liam. Vampires. Fangs and claws and blood.

Voices that wouldn't stop shouting in his head. Dark desires that could never be satisfied.

Desires that just grew worse as the blood flowed. Urges to hurt, to kill, to destroy.

It's not me anymore. I can't stop. Help me. Help me!

Jane wrenched her mouth away from Liam. Alerac yanked his hand back at the same instant.

And Liam fell. He slammed face-first into the floor.

She swiped her hand over her mouth, trying desperately to banish his taste and those terrible, twisted memories. She'd seen Liam hurting so many people. Humans and vampires and werewolves.

He'd hid his darkness for so many years.

No longer.

His heart was gone. His body was still. Liam was dead. Killed by his alpha's hand.

Jane looked up at Alerac. He stood there, bleeding, chest heaving, staring at her with the eyes of an enraged beast.

Part of her was afraid of him. *He'd taken the heart straight from Liam's chest.*

Alerac stepped toward her.

Her own heart raced faster.

His nostrils twitched.

He smells my fear. Oh, crap. "Alerac—"

But he'd whirled away from her. He stalked outside. Other werewolves were there. When had they gathered?

"It's done." His voice was flat. "The traitor is dead."

Ryan's fingers brushed down her arm. "Are you okay?"

She was. She just needed to talk with Alerac. To make him understand how she felt. "I need Alerac." Jane stepped toward him.

But the visions from Liam's head—those images of blood and pain and torture, flooded through her once more. She tried to stop them, but it was as if a dam had broken. The images wouldn't stop. They slammed through her, over and over again.

Was this what it was like for him? She could feel her sanity draining away.

She tried to call out to Alerac again, but couldn't.

Jane didn't hit the floor when she fell.

Her brother was there to catch her.

But there was nothing to stop the bloody visions that filled her mind.

CHAPTER ELEVEN

She thought he was a monster.

Fitting, considering that was exactly what Alerac was.

I killed Liam. Alerac had done what was necessary. Liam had been a menace, turning on his own kind, attacking Jane.

And when I killed him, I could have sworn I saw relief flash in his eyes.

"Jane?"

He frowned at the note of concern he heard in Ryan's voice. Alerac glanced back and saw Jane being cradled in her brother's arms.

Jane's eyes were closed, her long lashes dark against her pale cheeks.

"I think she fainted," Ryan muttered. He shook her gently. "Jane?"

"Vampires faint?" Zoe asked. "Here I thought blood-suckers were tougher than that." But a thread of concern had entered her voice, too.

Fear uncurled within Alerac. Fear, when he'd forced that emotion away for so long. But Jane seemed to be unlocking all of his emotions. The good and the bad. Helpless, he went back to her.

Had Jane fainted because she realized she was bound to a monster? To a man with a heart just as dark as Lorcan's?

He took her from Ryan. "Jane?"

She didn't stir.

She had blood on her clothes. On her skin.

"I'll take care of her," he said. He would. Always.

He cast a hard stare around the area. The witch was dead. Dammit, he'd needed her. He'd had plans for her. Now she was gone. *Maybe I can find another witch.* But her kind wasn't exactly thick on the ground, especially the powerful witches. "Take care of her," he ordered his men as he inclined his head toward the woman's still body.

Ryan glanced over at her bloody form. "She had no magic to help us."

"She didn't deserve to die!" From Zoe. Her cheeks were flushed. "She thought she was just getting to live, then Liam took that all away! She had hope, and he destroyed it."

Liam had taken much away from them.

No more.

Alerac turned and began to carry his precious burden up the stairs.

"What about Lorcan?" Ryan shouted after him.

Alerac paused. Until he found a way to break the link between Jane and Lorcan, there was nothing that could be done. "He lives." That was all he could say. "No one goes after him without my express command." Because any attack would hurt Jane, and that he could not allow. "If anyone catches his scent on our land, alert me immediately."

He left the others and carried Jane into the bathroom upstairs. The shower there was huge, easily big enough to accommodate them both.

"Jane?" Why hadn't her eyes opened?

He held her with one arm, positioning her against the glass door of the shower. He stripped her, wanting that blood-stained clothing away from her delicate skin.

Her lashes began to flutter.

He stilled at once. "I'm just taking care of you." Her fear was the last thing he wanted.

Jane's eyes opened fully. "He was crazy."

Alerac shook his head.

"I-I saw it. In his memories. The more blood he took, the more darkness ate away at him. Liam tried to hold on to his sanity, for so long, but he knew he was losing the battle."

"He never said…" Alerac began.

"His father went mad, didn't he?"

Alerac nodded. Some werewolves could turn feral. The most dangerous of their kind.

"He saw it happen," Jane whispered. Her hands rose and curled around Alerac's shoulders. "He saw it, and so did I. He knew the same fate was happening to him, and he thought that if he could just become immortal, like you, he'd have a different fate."

The drumming of Alerac's heart seemed to echo in his ears. "He drank vampire blood for me. To help me search for you. To avenge our pack." From the vampire attack that had nearly wiped them out so long ago. Lorcan's attack.

"No." Jane shook her head as her fingers tightened around his shoulders. "He did it for himself. Because he thought the blood would make him strong enough to fight the urges he had, but, after a while, it just made everything worse."

If Liam had been sick, Alerac should have known.

"He loved you," Jane whispered. "And he hated you."

His jaw locked. "You only had a few sips of his blood. You can't know all of this." She *couldn't* know it. Jane hadn't even gotten Alerac's memories until she'd slept.

A faint line was between her brows. "I think I'm stronger. *Your* blood made me stronger. Because I could see everything. From the first drop of blood that hit my tongue, I could *see*."

He wasn't sure why, but Alerac felt like those words were a warning. "Then maybe you should drink from me again. That way, you can fully *see* the monster before you." What the hell was he saying? He didn't want her to see him that way.

Did he?

Alerac stepped away from her. He'd stripped her down to her bra and underwear. He tried not to notice the delicate temptation of her body. Failed.

He leaned into the shower and yanked on the water. Then he stripped without looking at her.

He put his hands on the shower's glass door. "Why did you faint?" *Because of what I am?*

"His memories were too much. I couldn't shut them out any other way, so I guess I just shut down."

Alerac nodded. But he knew her words weren't the total truth. "You were afraid of me."

"Alerac…"

With a twisted smile, he glanced over at her. "You still are."

He climbed into the shower, and the rushing water poured over him.

The blood washed away. If only it were so easy to wash all the sins from his soul.

Then Jane was there. Naked, entering the shower with him. The water slickened her skin. Steam floated in the air around them.

"I am afraid of you," Jane confessed.

She was trying to break him.

"And I'm afraid of myself. Since I've met you, I've changed." Her body brushed against him.

If the woman was so scared, she needed to be stepping back. Not getting closer. Because in another few seconds, he'd be grabbing her.

He didn't plan to let go.

"I'm not the same woman you found in that bar. I-I still don't remember Keira, not really. But I've seen her, through your eyes." Her lips pressed together. "It's more than that, though. I'm stronger than I realized. *You* make me strong."

That was bullshit. She'd always been strong. Someone weak didn't trade her life for another's.

"I know that I'm going to keep changing. I'm not going to be fully Jane, not fully Keira, but something in the middle. That scares me." Then she made a mistake.

She touched him.

Wet, silken flesh.

His cock was already erect and aching. The too-big shower suddenly seemed too small.

"And you scare me, too. Because I know that you're dangerous."

Not to her, dammit, never to *her*.

"You make me feel so much. Desire. Need." She stood on her tip-toes and pressed her lips to his. "When I'm with you, I feel like you belong to me."

He did. Had, from the moment he first saw her.

"And I belong to you."

He pushed her against the tiled wall. "You do." He didn't care what twisted magic Lorcan had spun. Jane was his. In life. And beyond death.

He wouldn't let her go. He'd find a way to break that spell or curse or whatever the hell it was.

He'd find a way.

Jane's fingers slid down his body. Curled around his aroused flesh as he kissed her beneath the rough spray of the shower. His cock jerked at her touch. He was so ready for her. Always, for her. She stroked him, pumping his flesh, bringing his arousal to a harder, sharper, desperate edge.

Enough.

He lifted her up against that tile. Took her breast into his mouth. Licked and sucked and when she moaned, it was the sweetest sound he'd ever heard.

Her pleasure.

He kissed a path to her other breast. Her legs curled around his hips, and she positioned his cock right at the entrance to her sex.

"Now, Alerac, I need you *now.*"

He drove into her. Her silken heat covered him, straining around his length. His hands had flattened on the tile behind her. Their eyes were on level now. He stared at her.

In her gaze, Alerac saw every dream that he'd ever had.

Saw *her*.

He withdrew and thrust. Again and again. But he didn't make the rhythm rough and wild. Not this time. This time, he kept a stranglehold on his control. This time, he wanted to prove that he could be more than the savage who went wild for her.

His cock angled over her clit as he thrust. Her breaths came faster, harder. Her nails pressed into his shoulders. And her gaze held his.

His cock swelled even more. He drove deep.

Kissed her. Stroked her with his tongue and his lips, and she came around him, shuddering, her sex quivering along his length.

He held his body still as she came, loving the feel of her pleasure, and then, only when she was sated, he carried her from the shower. Her legs were still wrapped around his hips. His cock was still in the paradise of her body.

He lowered her onto the bed.

"Alerac?"

He smiled at her. "You make me happy." As few things in this world ever had.

Jane blinked at him, and her gaze seemed to soften. Then she smiled. "You make me...happy, too."

He kissed her again.

Started to thrust. Still not too hard, not too wild. He wanted her to come again. Endlessly. He wanted to show her all that he could give to her. Wanted to prove that their life together could be good.

If she gave him a chance.

If she wouldn't fear him.

Her heels pushed into his lower back. "Alerac, I want *everything.*" And her sex clamped around him, her delicate inner muscles tightening.

For an instant, he paused.

"Everything," she said once more, her voice a sensual demand. Then she arched toward him.

He put his hand between their bodies. Stroked her, pushed right when he knew her need was centered most.

He forced his control to hold. Forced it—

She came.

He shattered. No, his control shattered. He thrust fast and furiously now, determined to claim her, every single bit of her. When the pleasure hit him, it consumed Alerac, wiping away his past and his future. Wiping away everything.

But his Jane.

You make me happy.

He would fight for that happiness. Battle a hundred vampires. Slay any beast in his path.

As long as that path led to her.

***

He was dying.

Ryan could feel death coming. Death wasn't cold. Wasn't some icy touch. Death burned and twisted and cut, destroying him from the inside out.

He'd known that his time was coming. The pain had been growing.

Every moment, it had been his companion.

Lorcan and his twisted deals. He'd connected Ryan to his sister all right, a connection that had eaten away at him for too long.

He coughed, choking, and wasn't surprised to see blood come from his mouth.

"What's happening to you?"

Zoe. Whenever he turned around, she seemed to be there, watching him with her big, dark eyes.

"Nothing." *Death.* There was no point in telling her. The witch had been clear on what he needed.

A caged beast—that sure seemed to be Zoe. And it wasn't the first time that he'd heard that particular line. Lorcan had told him—when he

tracked the SOB down fifty years ago —
something similar. That his freedom lay with a
beast bound by chains that no one could see.

Knowing Lorcan's twisted streak, it had
figured that the beast in question was a werewolf.

Zoe was the only werewolf he'd ever
encountered who couldn't fully shift.

But if he bit her, she'd be destroyed.

For once, he'd do the right thing. He'd keep
his fangs away from her.

He coughed again. But he caught the blood in
his fist so she wouldn't see it. Then he turned
away from her, smearing it on his jeans. "I'm
going to check in the woods. Make sure that
Lorcan isn't around."

"The pack is patrolling —" Zoe began.

"And I'm going to patrol, too," he said
gruffly.

Lorcan. He'd wanted to help his sister defeat
their old clan leader, but he wasn't going to be
any use to her.

A brother found, then lost, all so suddenly.

Maybe she'd grieve for him.

Maybe she wouldn't.

He didn't look back at Zoe. She was too
much of a temptation to him.

He was just passing two twisted pine trees
when Zoe grabbed him. She spun him back
around to face her. "I can smell your blood."

Shifter nose. He inclined his head. "Good for you. Now do us both a favor…*stay away from me.*"

"The pain's worse."

He didn't reply. He didn't feel like lying anymore.

"Is this really what you want?" She asked him, tilting back her head and letting that heavy curtain of hair fall over her shoulders. "To just crawl off into the woods and die? Is that what you want for your sister? For her to stumble over your body?"

He wrapped his hands around her. *Dammit, mistake.* Because touching her flooded him with a dark need. "What I want," Ryan managed to choke out, "is to sink my teeth into your throat."

"Because I'm your cure?"

"Because I want to taste you."

She blinked at him.

Control. Control. Control. "But for once in my life, I'm trying to do the right thing." He moved her out of his way. Then he forced his fingers to stop touching her. To just let her go. "I'm not going to destroy you."

"The witch didn't say that you'd destroy me. Just my beast." Her laugh was brittle. "The beast in me hasn't ever been anything to brag about." Her hands lifted. Claws sprouted from her fingertips. "This is about all I've got. Claws and some enhanced strength. The others never wanted me here. They didn't think I belonged in the pack."

He ignored the pain. Just like always. Strange but, when he'd touched her, the pain had seemed to lessen. It was sure back full force now. "Alerac wants you here."

"Alerac is still trying to atone for the sins he committed against your sister. He tries to save everyone now. Finn…" Sadness flickered across her face. "Finn was my friend. The others here only tolerate me because Alerac tells them to do it. I'm not one of them, and *they know it.*"

He backed away from her. His heart seemed to be squeezing, held tight in a fist of fire. "And what is it that you want from me?"

Her lashes lowered, concealing her gaze. "I've heard the stories. When your sister bit Alerac, he changed. Became even more powerful. I've seen that power with my own eyes."

Her scent had wrapped around him. Lush. Woman.

"If you bite me, I might lose my beast."

Um, might? Based on what the witch had said, that was more of a definite.

"But maybe I can become something else. Something even more powerful."

Hell. She needed to get away from him. "Do you want to turn out like Liam?"

Zoe flinched.

"Because that could happen. Vamp blood isn't exactly the safest drug out there." For many, that was exactly what it was—a drug. An addiction.

An addiction to power and darkness.

Do the right thing. Dammit, he was. For once. "Go back to your pack. Protect the alpha. And just forget you ever met me."

Ryan spun turned away from her. Hesitated. "Please tell Jane I said good-bye." He hadn't used their link to touch her mind again. Because he hadn't wanted her to see his certainty of death.

So he'd kept a wall between them, even though he'd felt her reach out to him several times. If he'd let her in, she might have felt his pain. He didn't want her suffering as he did.

He hadn't protected her before. He was trying to, now.

Ryan swiped away the blood that dripped from his lips. Then, just as Zoe said, he crawled away to die.

***

Jane opened her eyes and stared up at the ceiling. Darkness had fallen, she could *feel* it. An instinctive awareness.

Alerac was beside her, his body a warm and solid weight against her. He'd wrapped his arm around her stomach, pulling her close.

She had more of his memories. So many more.

I'll take his punishment. She'd had visions of that terrible night again.

But Jane still didn't remember the actual punishment that she'd endured. And she sure didn't remember any last minute deal that she'd made with Lorcan, agreeing to bind their lives.

But I know how to remember that deal.

Her memories were gone. Lost. Lorcan's weren't. She could retrieve his memories just as she'd retrieved Alerac's. All she needed was some blood.

Lorcan's blood.

Her head turned. She stared at Alerac. In sleep, he didn't look quite so fierce. The hard lines of his face were smoothed some, his hair tousled.

Her fingers lifted and brushed lightly through his hair. Then she bent and pressed a light kiss to his cheek.

Alerac's eyes opened. The brightness didn't shock her anymore. She'd seen his memories of the attack.

He'd blocked most of the pain. And instead of seeing darkness, he'd chosen to see her.

As long as Lorcan lived, he would be a threat to Alerac. Lorcan had wanted Alerac's destruction two centuries ago.

He wanted it now.

"He's not going to stop," Jane whispered.

A faint furrow appeared between Alerac's brows.

"Lorcan will keep coming," she continued. Just like the monsters in all the movies she'd watched on Saturday nights. "We have to stop *him.*"

Alerac sat up, and the sheets fell into a tangle near his waist. "We can't. If he dies, then *you* die."

Her fingers rose and stroked over his tattoo. "Tell me why you got this." She knew—she'd seen it in his memories. Yet it seemed important for him to tell her on his own.

His heart raced beneath her fingers. "It's my symbol—forever. Eternity.

An endless knot.

"It's…for you," he continued, voice roughening. "A design to show that I am bound to you, forever, that I would search until I found you."

"You found me," she whispered.

"And I won't let you go. But I won't kill Lorcan because I can't hurt you."

She'd been afraid he would say that. "What if Lorcan comes after your pack? What if hunts them?" As he'd done before.

When he killed Alerac's family. She'd seen that memory. The terrible carnage that Alerac had found when he'd returned to his home and found death waiting, courtesy of Lorcan.

Alerac shook his head. "We can defend ourselves."

No, they couldn't. "Not if you aren't willing to kill the one attacking you."

His hand slid under her jaw. "No one hurts you. You will not suffer again for me or mine—"

She knew her smile was sad. "Oh, Alerac, are you still blaming yourself?"

Confusion flickered over his face.

Jane pulled away from him. She climbed from the bed. Dressed with fumbling fingers. *Hurry, hurry.*

"I am to blame." His words were slow. "You suffered for me."

Enough. She put her hands on her hips and faced him. "I suffered for me. I made the choice. Not you. It was all me." Because she wasn't some child to have others determine her life. Not then, and not now. It was still her choice. "I couldn't stand by and watch you die."

"Your memory…it's back?"

"No, your memories are." She'd seen herself clearly through his eyes. Heard her own whispered confession of love. "Watching you die would have destroyed me."

And if she didn't do something about Lorcan, the same fate would wait for her. *Lorcan wasn't going to give up.* She turned from Alerac and paced toward the window.

She stared into the darkness. When would another attack come?

Her hand lifted and rubbed over her heart. It was aching.

No, it was burning.

Pain suddenly stole her voice, and Jane doubled over. Her head hit the window, and glass shattered.

"Jane!" Alerac was there in an instant, pulling her toward him.

The burn just grew worse. And, in her mind, she could see the sudden image of her brother. "Ryan," she whispered. She hadn't touched his mind fully again, not since that one time when he'd sent his message to her, but Jane knew that she was reaching him in that pain-filled moment.

"What's happening?" Alerac demanded. His hands were so gentle on her.

Jane forced her head to lift. "He's dying."

No surprise was in Alerac's gaze.

No hope, either.

Jane pulled in a heavy breath. Blood was dripping from a cut over her right eyebrow. The heat from the night drifted in from that broken glass. "I'm not going to let him go like this." She'd just found him. To lose him now — *no.*

"What will you do?" Alerac asked her. "Trade Zoe's life for his?"

She wasn't interested in a trade. "Lorcan can end this all."

She just had to find him.

Even if she had to do it on her own.

Jane yanked away from Alerac. "I'm sorry." Then she leapt right through the window. More glass shattered around her. This time, she hadn't slowed down long enough to open the window. She'd just gone right through the glass. *I'm stronger now.*

"*Jane!*"

Her knees didn't buckle when she landed. She didn't hesitate on the ground. She could smell her brother's blood, and she followed that scent, running hard and fast through the woods.

She wouldn't be the only one who wanted to see Ryan at the end. After all of his games, after all of his sick plans, Jane thought Lorcan might want to witness the sight of her brother dying, too.

Footsteps thundered behind her. Alerac. She'd known that he would give chase.

But what Alerac didn't know…*I'm stronger than he is right now.* Stronger and faster. His blood fueled her and power pulsed beneath her skin. So her legs pumped faster. The trees passed her in a blur, and she tracked the scent of her brother's blood deep into the woods.

***

Ryan hit the ground. A stone slammed into his cheek, and he felt a bone break.

He couldn't go any farther.

Didn't want to.

When he breathed—a jagged exhale—smoke drifted from his lips.

He was truly burning from the inside.

He'd been weak a moment before. He'd thought of his sister. Just a flash, and he'd been *in* her mind.

He'd tried to pull back, but she'd had the link then.

She'd known what was happening to him.

His fingers sank into the mud. He'd tried to get away from her. Away from everyone. But—

A twig snapped behind him.

Ryan forced his body to roll over.

She was there. Fate was cruel, giving him this last sight on earth.

Zoe shook her head as she crept out of the trees and toward the small clearing. "Are you done running? Are you ready to see reason?"

Reason? Reason wasn't about destroying someone like her so that he could live.

She took another step toward. "Let me do this—" But she broke off as her head jerked up. She started to whirl back toward the trees.

Ryan tried to yell a warning.

He couldn't.

Blood flew from his lips. Blood and smoke.

And blood flew from Zoe's neck. Because Lorcan had just appeared near Zoe. Lorcan had sliced his fangs across her throat.

As Ryan lay there, helpless to do anything but *watch*, Lorcan dropped Zoe to the ground. A pain-filled moan slipped from her lips.

"Couldn't have her ruining things for me, now could I?" Lorcan murmured as he wiped the blood from his lips. "Not when I've been waiting so long for this particular show." Lorcan smiled.

Zoe wouldn't be his last sight on earth.

The last image that Ryan would see — it would be the devil.

CHAPTER TWELVE

Jane burst from the trees, and she slammed her body into Lorcan's. "Stay away from him!" Fury drove her, just amping up the power in her body.

She and Lorcan hit the ground, then they rolled in a tangle of limbs. Rocks and branches cut into her skin, and when they stopped their mad tumble, she was on top of Lorcan.

The SOB was grinning up at her. "Knew you'd be here, too," he said, sounding *pleased*. "Knew it...we both wanted to see him die."

"I'm not here to watch my brother die." She held Lorcan's hands against the ground. From the corner of her eye, she saw Zoe.

Zoe wasn't dead. Not yet. The scent of the werewolf's blood filled Jane's nostrils. Maybe Zoe *should* be dead, but she wasn't.

Zoe was crawling, dragging her body toward Ryan.

"Of course, you are." Lorcan didn't fight her grip. Just kept grinning. "There's no other way for this to end."

"We'll see about that," Jane said, then she sank her teeth into his throat.

Lorcan yelled and tried to throw her off him. She held on tight. She drank.

And his memories came to her.

***

"You think you're brave…" Lorcan's voice. Booming.

Jane saw her image, a pale woman with her wrists bound and her ankles chained.

"You aren't," he snarled at her. "Your lover will be dead long before you're free."

"You promised that you wouldn't kill him!" Fear flared in her eyes.

"I won't kill him. I'll just make him beg for death."

Jane saw herself try to struggle out of the bonds.

"And I never promised not to kill your brother."

She stopped fighting the bonds.

Lorcan walked around her. They were…in a dark room. Stone for a floor. Stone for the walls. She'd been cut, deep slices at her wrists, and dried blood covered her hands.

"You were a traitor, so I have to expect that Ryan will be one, too." He bent near her, brushing his mouth beside her cheek. "How much shall I make him suffer?"

"Don't!"

He laughed. "Do you want to save him? Do you want to make me a deal, the same way you bargained for the life of that werewolf?"

"Please," the word was a ragged breath. "Spare Ryan. He didn't know that I was with Alerac. He had nothing to—"

"I can make him into nothing. I can stake him out at dawn. I can drain him. I can turn him into ash that drifts on the wind."

The big, wooden door opened. A woman stepped inside.

"Ah, Shonna, so good of you to join us." Lorcan didn't look back at her. His stare remained on his prey. "What will you give me, lost little Keira, if I let Ryan live to see you free once more?"

The desolation eased in her eyes. Hope brightened her stare. "What do you want?"

"He begged me to free you. Offered to trade *anything* for your safety."

A blood red tear tracked through the dirt on her cheek.

"Bind your life to mine," Lorcan said.

His words were chilling. She saw the shiver rake her body.

"Agree to the link, a link that will last until death for us, and I'll let your brother live."

She nodded.

He shook his finger. "No, that's not how it works. You have to say the words. Doesn't she, Shonna?" He looked over his shoulder at the woman with a long braid of red hair. A woman with a knife in her hand.

"Yes," Shonna whispered. Then she began to whisper the words of a spell.

The bite scars on Shonna's neck twisted the witch's skin.

Lorcan's focused shifted away from the witch. "Your werewolf will be long gone before you're truly free. You won't be betraying him," Lorcan added as he brushed her hair over her shoulders. "You'll be saving your brother."

Another shudder shook her form. "I-I'll bind to you, until death."

At those words, the witch rushed forward with her knife. She drove that knife into Keira's chest. More blood joined the dirt and grime that covered her.

"The bind will start the moment you escape your prison, when your lungs fill with their first taste of new air," the witch's words seemed to echo with power. "The bond will continue, through blood and pain, until one of you dies."

Then Lorcan took the knife. He licked the blood away from the blade. "Death will be a very long time coming."

***

"Get the hell away from her!" Alerac bellowed.

His cry had Jane jerking up. The images vanished.

And Lorcan was able to toss her aside.

In the next instant, Lorcan was on his feet. "She was the one to come for me," Lorcan taunted. "I guess our link is stronger than she'd have you believe."

Jane spat out the blood in her mouth. She hated having any part of him in her, but now Jane understood.

She'd agreed to the trade. Lorcan had been right, she'd willingly bound herself to him. "You bastard."

Lorcan turned to look at her.

"You said that you'd let my brother live!"

Lorcan shook his finger at her. "No, I said he'd live to see you free. You're free. He's dead." With a smirk, he glanced toward Ryan's form.

But Ryan wasn't alone on the ground. Zoe had made her way to him. She'd shoved her wrist over Ryan's mouth. With tears streaming down her cheeks, Zoe cried out, "Jane…make him…bite!"

Alerac rushed to Zoe's side. "Get away from him! You know what will happen if he bites you!"

Her beast would die.

"I'm…already d-dying…" Zoe's voice was weaker. Probably because she was missing a big part of her throat. There was so much blood. "Let me…h-help…" Her gaze found Jane's. "Make him b-bite…"

Lorcan stalked toward Zoe and Alerac. "It doesn't work that way, bitch. You don't get to save him. No one does."

His claws flew toward Zoe's neck.

Jane screamed.

Alerac caught Lorcan's hands in a tight grip.

Lorcan didn't back away. He leaned in toward Alerac. "How are you going to stop me? How are you going to stop me from doing anything? You can't hurt me. Because, if you do, you hurt *her*."

Alerac's gaze flew to Jane.

"Tighten your grip a bit more," Lorcan taunted. "Break my wrist. Break *her* wrist."

Alerac became as still as stone.

"M-make him bite…" Zoe begged.

Jane focused on the female werewolf. Zoe only had a few moments left.

"C-can't shift to heal…" Zoe whispered. "Could never…s-survive…"

Jane straightened her shoulders. *Bite, Ryan.* She attempted to find a link to his mind. She was trying desperately to reach out to him, but she couldn't connect. She could only feel an icy touch, a too deep cold, seeming to emanate from him.

Bite.

Zoe's wrist was still over Ryan's mouth. Her eyes were sagging closed.

Thud. Thud. Zoe's heart was giving its last few beats. Jane's enhanced hearing barely picked up the feeble sounds.

"What are you doing?" Lorcan had torn away from Alerac. His eyes were on Jane. "What the hell do you think you're doing?"

"Saving my brother."

"He *can't* be saved! He's dead! He's—"

Zoe gasped.

Jane smiled. "He's not dead yet. He's feeding."

Lorcan lunged toward Jane. Before he could grab her, Alerac was in his path once again.

"You won't ever hurt her again," Alerac vowed.

Lorcan staggered to a stop. "Of course, I will. I'll hurt her again and again. Watch and see." Then he lifted up his claws—and plunged them into his own chest.

Blood poured from the matching wound that instantly appeared on Jane's body.

Lorcan smiled his sadistic grin. "I can hurt her anytime I want. From anywhere I want. That was all part of the spell. Pain for pain. Life for life."

Lorcan hadn't driven the claws into his heart—because he didn't want to die. He just wanted her to suffer.

Alerac yanked the claws out of Lorcan's chest. "Stop it," he gritted.

Jane's blood dripped onto the ground.

"I'll stop hurting her," Lorcan agreed, voice sly and silken, "once you're gone, wolf. Get the hell out of here. Leave Jane, and I won't hurt her again."

Lie.

Alerac glanced over his shoulder at Jane.

She shook her head. "We both know that's bullshit." She ignored the pain in her chest. Or, at least, she didn't let the pain send her to her knees. "You leave, and he'll go after your pack."

"I'll go after them anyway." Lorcan admitted easily. "Dogs need death. And *he*," he swiped his claws over Alerac's chest. Alerac didn't even fight back. Alerac *let* the bastard attack him. "He won't stop me. He can't. Not if he wants to keep his precious *a rúnsearc* safe."

A rúnsearc.

Alerac had said that meant vampire.

He'd lied to her.

What it really meant was...*secret love.* She knew that, now. Because she had Alerac and Lorcan's understanding of the language.

Alerac had been telling her how he felt, all along. She hadn't realized...

Alerac hadn't just been using her two centuries before. *He loves me.*

She ran to him and yanked him away from Lorcan's attack. Jane forced Alerac to face her.

His fierce gaze locked on hers. "There's a way," he said to Jane. "I know there is. I just have to find it."

"If I take those wolf eyes of yours, will you grow another set?" Lorcan asked, voice curious. "I can't wait to find out." His voice hardened as he said, "In case you missed the news, I have the power here. All of it. You can't hurt me, not without hurting her. You can't do a damn thing to me, but I can sure as fuck enjoy hurting *you.*"

Alerac's shoulders straightened. She knew that he'd take whatever pain Lorcan gave to him—and not fight back.

For me.

His pack would suffer.

For me.

In the end, Alerac would lose his life.

For me.

She wasn't going to let that happen. "It was my choice before," Jane whispered to him.

Alerac shook his head.

"It's my choice now." She pushed onto her toes. Pressed her lips against his. "I love you."

Then she backed away from him.

"No, Jane," Alerac began. "you can't—"

"Hold him, Ryan."

Alerac's eyes widened. He glanced over his shoulder.

Ryan wasn't on the ground anymore. Wasn't spitting up blood. He was on his feet, and in an instant, he'd lunged toward Alerac. Ryan wrapped his hands around Alerac. Held him tight.

Jane knew her brother wouldn't be able to hold Alerac for long.

But she didn't need a long time. After all, it only took seconds to die. She bent and grabbed a broken branch near her feet. Good thing there were plenty of tree branches lying around. And all you needed to stake a vampire was a chunk of wood. "The deal's over, Lorcan. Consider the bond broken."

Lorcan's eyes widened.

They were still wide when she rushed toward him and drove that branch right through his heart.

Didn't see that coming, did you, bastard?

***

"*No!*" The cry ripped from Alerac. He tossed Ryan aside. Raced toward Jane.

The wood went straight through Lorcan's body, shoving out of his back. Blood covered the vamp as his knees gave way and he hit the ground.

Alerac grabbed Jane before she could fall, too.

"*A rúnsearc*, what have you done?" Her chest was soaked with blood. Her breath barely wheezed out. "*Why?*"

"B-because y-you wouldn't…ever h-hurt me…"

"So you decided to end things yourself? You can't do this!" Rage and grief twisted inside him, and destroyed any sane thought. "I won't let you go! Dammit, *no!*"

Blood trickled from her mouth. Her eyes stared up at him. "Love…"

"No!" He pulled her against his chest. Rocked her with mindless motions of his body. "Don't tell me that you love me. Don't say that you love me while your heart is—"

She wasn't moving.

He couldn't breathe. "J-Jane?"

He tilted back her head. Her eyes were closed.

"Jane, don't do this!"

His hold on her was too hard. He had to ease his grip or he'd bruise her. He couldn't bruise Jane. He couldn't hurt Jane. He needed her too much. She had to stay with him. He couldn't make it through any more years without her.

"Lorcan's dead."

Ryan's voice. Alerac's head snapped up. His gaze narrowed on the vampire. The one who'd held him back. If Ryan hadn't grabbed him, then

Alerac could have stopped Jane. He could have *saved* her.

No, no, I'll still save her. She's not gone. Not yet. She'll come back to me.

"We should burn his body," Ryan continued. "Just to make fucking sure."

"No!" Alerac's roar. If they burned Lorcan, then they would burn Jane.

Ryan swallowed. He stared right back at Alerac. Grief was in the vamp's eyes. "She knew that you wouldn't kill him, that you'd let your pack die, that *you'd* die, for her."

Yes, in an instant, he would have given his life for her.

"She chose to save you instead. Just like before." Ryan's lips twisted, but there was no humor there. Only pain. "Looks like two hundred years didn't change the way that she felt about you, memory or no memory."

The drumming of Alerac's heartbeat was too loud. A red haze covered his vision. That haze was blood.

Jane's blood.

Jane.

"You aren't burning him," Alerac said. HIs words sounded hoarse, as if they'd been scraped from his throat. "You aren't burning *her.*"

Alerac's gaze flew back to Jane. He couldn't look away. Jane had saved him, too many times.

It was his turn to save her. He *had* to save her. There wasn't any other option for him.

Without her, he didn't want to walk this earth.

Without her, it wouldn't be *safe* for him to walk this earth.

"She just needs blood," he said. His words were ragged. So was his breath. "Blood heals. That's all she needs."

Ryan's footsteps shuffled closer. "Blood won't bring back the dead."

"She's not *dead.*"

"Yes, she is." A soft voice — Zoe?

His head turned. He saw her standing, pale, trembling, just behind Ryan.

"She's not breathing, Alerac," Zoe told him with pity in her eyes. "She —"

"She was in the ground for two centuries!" Alerac yelled back. "A witch put a spell on her then. She didn't need breath. She can still *live!*"

He had to make her live. He cut his wrist, sliced it quickly with his claws, then dripped the blood into Jane's mouth. Then he massaged her neck — *she's warm, that means she lives* — as he attempted to force the blood down her throat.

"We're linked," Alerac whispered. "She made me more than just a beast. I made her more than just a vampire." *Please don't leave me. Please.* "She's still *here.*"

He held her tight. He gave her his blood. "I love you, Jane," he whispered. He told her that truth again and again.

But her eyes didn't open.

And the beast within him broke just as the man did.

***

Ryan felt as if his own heart had been cut out. Alerac wouldn't let his sister go. He clung to her too tightly. Had to hold her close constantly. Alerac had finally left the woods moments before, with Jane still held in his arms.

"Are we going to...to lose him?" Zoe's voice. She came toward him, a torch in her hands. Her movements were slow, her body still trembled, but her gaze was unflinching as it met his.

She saved my life.

By sacrificing her beast.

The fire in his chest was gone. The pain, the certainty of death—all gone.

Because of her.

How was he supposed to repay a debt like that?

"Will he s-survive losing her?" Zoe asked. Her voice broke a bit. Her throat was almost fully healed. He knew the catch in her words came from grief, not pain.

Ryan wasn't sure that Alerac would survive. But one thing he *did* know…he had to burn Lorcan's body. That had been Jane's last order to him.

*Bite…*her whisper had floated through his mind, and he'd found himself sinking his teeth into Zoe's arm.

Then…

Stop Alerac. Hold him.

He'd been at Alerac's back in the next moment.

Burn Lorcan. Nothing can remain.

He took the torch from Zoe. They'd waited until Alerac left for this last act.

But…when he burned Lorcan, would Jane's body turn to ash, too? He knew that was what Alerac feared.

"Go to him," he said quietly. "Make sure…" *That he doesn't jump into the flames if Jane's body sparks fire. Make sure that he doesn't turn on his pack as the rage consumes him.*

Zoe nodded and she hurried away.

Ryan stood over Lorcan's body, staring down at the vampire who'd ruined so many lives.

But now, now that vampire would burn in hell.

"My sister's free of you," Ryan told him, voice thick. "You can't ever hurt her again."

He lifted the torch. He'd wait just a few more minutes so that Zoe could get to Alerac. Just a few minutes more.

***

"Alerac, stop!"

He didn't stop. He kept walking, numb, holding Jane tight. Had he ever told her how beautiful she was? When she smiled, it was the most perfect sight he'd ever witnessed.

He wished that she had smiled more.

He'd wanted to spend an eternity at her side.

He'd been given just days.

Zoe grabbed his arm. "Let her *go.*"

He couldn't, not yet.

"Ryan is burning Lorcan. You know it has to be done. He was so strong—"

His body tensed. "That will burn *her.*"

"Y-yes…"

He spun in an instant and rushed back through the woods. Ryan should know better. Ryan was her *brother.* He should want to keep her alive. Not give her to the flames. As he ran, Alerac kept Jane locked tightly in his arms. Was her body growing colder? No, no, it couldn't.

The smell of smoke teased his nose. "Stop!" Alerac bellowed.

Flames began to crackle.

"Stop!"

He burst into the clearing.

Ryan shook his head and lowered the torch. The fire caught the edge of Lorcan's shirt. Grazed over the vamp's skin. Then Lorcan *ignited*.

The flames spread instantly.

And Jane's body began to feel warmer.

"No," Alerac whispered. This couldn't happen. Things were supposed to end differently for them. He was going to protect her. Going to spend all of his life with her.

"Put her down before you burn!" Zoe cried.

But he just held Jane tighter.

"Things were going to be different," he whispered.

Lorcan was completely engulfed in flames. Jane's body was even warmer now.

"So different." He closed his eyes and bent his head. His lips brushed over her forehead.

Then he heard...it.

A soft thud.

A heart, beating again.

Breath whispered from lips that had been still moments before.

Alerac was afraid to look at Jane. What if his vision proved the other senses to be a lie? Better to stay this way, to just hope...

Has my sanity left already?

Without her, yes, he knew it had.

"Things will be different." That was *her* voice. Soft and husky and *hers*.

Helpless now, his lashes lifted.

Jane's pale lips tried to curve into a smile. "I could…sure use a little…more of the super blood y-you…have…"

He'd give her *anything*.

"Feel like…death warmed…over…" Jane told him.

She was trying to joke? When he'd just nearly lost his life? Because if he'd lost her, his life would not have been worth living. *I couldn't survive without her again.*

He lifted her higher. Her arms curled around his neck. Her fangs sank into his throat.

Alive. Alive. Alive!

"Jane?" Ryan sounded shocked. "Holy hell, *Jane!*"

Her mouth pulled away from Alerac's throat. She looked up at him. Stared deeply into Alerac's eyes. "I'm only bound…to you now."

He'd always be bound to her.

"You p-pulled me back." Her voice was gaining strength. Faint color filled her cheeks. "You gave me…some of the beast inside. Inside *me.*"

Not just vampire. Not just werewolf.

"His tie only lasted until death." Jane smiled. *The most beautiful sight.* "Yours lasted longer, and so did I."

Good. Because if she hadn't come back to him, Alerac would have followed her. He would have fuckin' fought death. Done anything — for her.

"I love you," he told her. He needed her to hear the words. Alerac needed to say them, even though love felt like far too tame of a description for the way he felt.

"I know, *a rúnsearc*," Jane told him, eyes bright with emotion. "I know."

A rúnsearc. Secret love. The love that had been in his heart from the moment he first saw her.

The love that would continue on in this world and beyond death.

He eased Jane to her feet. Her brother instantly grabbed her and held her tight.

Zoe wiped away tears. Alerac reached for the she-wolf, pulling her close.

"I-I'm not pack anymore," Zoe mumbled, "I should-"

"You're pack," he told her flatly. "You're family." And that was all that anyone needed to know. He owed Zoe a debt he could never repay.

A debt that Ryan could never repay, but he'd sure enjoy watching the vampire try.

Then Jane was coming back to him. Smiling. Breaking his heart with her beauty. Filling him with a hope that he hadn't dared to feel in far too long.

"I saw Lorcan's memories," Jane told him. "I knew death was the way to break the tie."

"You actually *died?*" Zoe's voice rose. "Then how did you come back?"

"Love," Jane said softly. "Love, and a bit of werewolf blood. It's damn powerful stuff."

Was she talking about werewolf blood being powerful? Or love?

"It can break any curse or spell." Jane rose onto her toes and brushed her lips over Alerac's. "It can survive anything."

She put her hand over his heart. The heart that beat for her, now and always.

Over her shoulder, Alerac saw Ryan cast a quick glance toward Zoe. There was so much emotion in the vamp's eyes. Emotion that was familiar to Alerac.

No, Zoe wasn't leaving the pack or the family that was being created.

A family with ties that had been forged in blood and death.

A family that now had a future.

"Take me home, wolf," Jane ordered him as her fingers stroked over his chest. "I'm ready to have that 'something different' you promised me."

He glanced toward the fire, but it was out now. Just smoke, drifting away.

Lorcan was gone. No more monsters to slay.

Well, at least not at that moment. Alerac was sure there would be more paranormal ass to kick eventually.

There always was.

But for now, he'd take his mate, the love that he could see in her eyes, and he'd enjoy the happiness that they had coming.

No more punishment.

No more death.

For them, it was time to be free. Time to *live*.

A werewolf and his vampire. Together.

Forever.

The End

###

A NOTE FROM THE AUTHOR

I hope that you enjoyed my latest "Bound" story. Thanks for taking the time to read Alerac and Jane's tale!

If you'd like to stay updated on my releases and sales, please join my newsletter list.

http://cynthiaeden.com/newsletter/

Again, thank you for reading SECRET ADMIRER.

Best,
Cynthia Eden
www.cynthiaeden.com

ABOUT THE AUTHOR

Award-winning author Cynthia Eden writes dark
tales of paranormal romance and romantic
suspense. She is a New York Times, USA Today,
Digital Book World, and IndieReader best-seller.
Cynthia is also a three-time finalist for the RITA®
award. Since she began writing full-time in 2005,
Cynthia has written over eighty novels and
novellas.

For More Information

- *cynthiaeden.com*
- *http://facebook.com/cynthiaedenfanpage*
- *http://twitter.com/cynthiaeden*

HER OTHER WORKS

Romantic Suspense
Lazarus Rising

- Never Let Go (Book One, Lazarus Rising)
- Keep Me Close (Book Two, Lazarus Rising)
- Stay With Me (Book Three, Lazarus Rising)
- Run To Me (Book Four, Lazarus Rising)
- Lie Close To Me (Book Five, Lazarus Rising)
- Hold On Tight (Book Six, Lazarus Rising)

Dark Obsession Series

- Watch Me (Dark Obsession, Book 1)
- Want Me (Dark Obsession, Book 2)
- Need Me (Dark Obsession, Book 3)
- Beware Of Me (Dark Obsession, Book 4)
- Only For Me (Dark Obsession, Books 1 to 4)

Mine Series

- Mine To Take (Mine, Book 1)
- Mine To Keep (Mine, Book 2)
- Mine To Hold (Mine, Book 3)
- Mine To Crave (Mine, Book 4)
- Mine To Have (Mine, Book 5)
- Mine To Protect (Mine, Book 6)
- Mine Series Box Set Volume 1 (Mine, Books 1-3)
- Mine Series Box Set Volume 2 (Mine, Books 4-6)

Other Romantic Suspense

- First Taste of Darkness
- Sinful Secrets
- Until Death
- Christmas With A Spy
- Secret Admirer

Paranormal Romance
Bad Things

- The Devil In Disguise (Bad Things, Book 1)
- On The Prowl (Bad Things, Book 2)
- Undead Or Alive (Bad Things, Book 3)
- Broken Angel (Bad Things, Book 4)
- Heart Of Stone (Bad Things, Book 5)
- Tempted By Fate (Bad Things, Book 6)
- Bad Things Volume One (Books 1 to 3)
- Bad Things Volume Two (Books 4 to 6)

- Bad Things Deluxe Box Set (Books 1 to 6)
- Wicked And Wild (Bad Things, Book 7)
- Saint Or Sinner (Bad Things, Book 8)

Bite Series

- Forbidden Bite (Bite Book 1)
- Mating Bite (Bite Book 2)

Blood and Moonlight Series

- Bite The Dust (Blood and Moonlight, Book 1)
- Better Off Undead (Blood and Moonlight, Book 2)
- Bitter Blood (Blood and Moonlight, Book 3)
- Blood and Moonlight (The Complete Series)

Purgatory Series

- The Wolf Within (Purgatory, Book 1)
- Marked By The Vampire (Purgatory, Book 2)
- Charming The Beast (Purgatory, Book 3)
- Deal with the Devil (Purgatory, Book 4)
- The Beasts Inside (Purgatory, Books 1 to 4)

Bound Series

- Bound By Blood (Bound Book 1)
- Bound In Darkness (Bound Book 2)
- Bound In Sin (Bound Book 3)
- Bound By The Night (Bound Book 4)
- Forever Bound (Bound, Books 1 to 4)
- Bound in Death (Bound Book 5)